NUMBER NEIGHBOR

KD ROBICHAUX
CC MONROE

Copyright © 2019 by KD Robichaux and CC Monroe

All rights reserved.

No part of this book may be reproduced in any form or by any electronic or mechanical means, including information storage and retrieval systems, without written permission from the author, except for the use of brief quotations in a book review.

To us, CC.
We did it.
#mombosses
<3, Tits

PROLOGUE

Owen

I watch her. Like I do every night. Parked in the driveway of the once-vacant house next door, just outside her bedroom window. I bought it after I followed her home one night, months ago and realized she likes to undress with her blinds open, knowing I'd kill anyone else who discovered that fact. I don't stay here though. No, I live in the top-floor penthouse in a downtown high-rise close to work.

The curvature of her lithe frame, sitting at just 5'6", is a whole foot shorter than me. Her breasts are lush and full; my entire hand could grip one and it would still overflow my palm. She must want to be watched, and that both benefits and infuriates me, because other men can lust over what I have deemed as mine—her. I will be the only man to watch, touch, and fuck her until mine is the only name she ever screams.

She isn't ready for that yet, and that's why I will

continue to watch her from her window every night. Touch myself while she does things that shouldn't turn me on but do. Like the way she stares at her naked body in the mirror. I can tell she is being self-critical, but really she has no idea what that slightly rounded belly does to me. When she runs her fingers over it, does she see something ugly? Because all I see is where I plan to put my baby in her once I make her mine. I can see it now, her gorgeous, thick thighs tightening around my hips as she tries to subdue the pleasure that courses through her. I want to fucking taste those pouty lips that she licks randomly. Bite them until they're swollen and red with the evidence of my ownership.

I pull out my cock; it stands tall and ready for attention. I pretend my hand is hers and she is nervously touching it for the first time. That body in there? That innocent, sexy woman? She's a virgin. I can practically smell it from here. I know when she touches me for the first time, my hard, angry-looking cock will frighten my woman, and I can't wait to teach her how to ride it.

"Fuck, turn around, baby." I swear my mind and body is in tune with hers, so much that I'm controlling her with my words. She turns, naked, her entire body facing me, and fuck if she isn't putting on a show for me.

She tilts her head slightly, reaching one hand behind her to move her hair to one side, her tits swaying slightly with the motion. She bites at her lip as she bends to grab her shirt from the bed.

I pick up speed, knowing she's about to cover that gorgeous form. Her slight bend seems slow and deliberate, her delectable ass rounding with her ninety-degree angle. "I will bend you over that bed, baby. Fuck you raw."

My orgasm comes on quickly, something that was

never a thing before I saw her. It usually takes a lot to get me off. Most women I've been with were worn out when I was done with them. I am an animal when I fuck, and I fuck hard—rigorously. The fact that just a few small movements and less than a minute can pass and she has my balls swelling with cum I want to unload in her, means this woman was made for only my pleasure.

"Look up. Let me see those beautiful green eyes. Come on, baby. I need it. Look at me." I know my windows are tinted and she won't be able to see me, but I can see her and that's all I need—a brief look to seal the deal.

She puts her top on, and right then, something falls off the vanity behind her and she turns around to pick it up, giving me a full view of her ass and bare pussy. I come then, my orgasm so harsh I see stars as I watch her look back out the window, and walk to them to shut her blinds before going to bed. I see her look out into the darkness before she fully closes them, and that last glimpse is timed with the last spurt of my cum—the same cum I wish was filling her.

"I love you. Good night, baby." I take a deep breath after her figure disappears from view, and my nightly stalking coming to an end. Knowing I will be back tomorrow, doesn't stop me from being slightly aggravated that I have to leave. One day soon, I will get inside her home, inside her, and I will show her every damn bit of my obsession with her.

I just have to find a way in.

CHAPTER 1

Ivy

"Did you read the Buzzfeed article I sent you?" Jenika asks as she leans her hip against my desk in the reception area of the private practice where we work. I glance up from my typing to see her scrolling on her phone, a slight smile on her face.

I lean back in my rolling chair, pulling my glasses off to rub the bridge of my nose between my thumb and index finger. "I haven't had a chance yet. I've been redoing Dr. Sage's appointment schedule all morning, since he wants to start closing earlier on Fridays."

She glances down at me. "A lot of work now, but think about how nice it'll be to get off at noon on Friday and then not have to be back at work until 9:00 a.m. Monday morning."

I lift my brows. "True story. That's like... five extra hours of weekend debauchery." I giggle, and she winks. But at the same time, I'll miss those extra five hours of catching secret glimpses of my handsome boss between patients.

"Exactly, girl. Speaking of—it's noon. Take lunch. I want you to read this shit and discuss," she entices, and I give in, pulling the clock sign out of my desk drawer and setting it to say I'll return at 1:00 p.m. Dr. Sage doesn't have another appointment until then anyway.

I grab my phone and Vera Bradley lunch kit out of the large bottom drawer of the sleek wooden desk I perch at forty hours a week, standing and wobbling on my new shiny black heels for a second.

"Still haven't gotten the hang of those bad boys yet?" she teases.

I grimace. "No, and I doubt I ever will. If the good doctor didn't pay me so freaking well, I'd tell him to shove the dress code up his fine-as-hell ass and find a new job just so I wouldn't have to wear these damn things." It's a total lie. He could pay me far less and I'd still wear whatever the hell he asked me to. Anything to please Dr. Sage.

"Yeah well, it's his fancy shmancy practice, and he has a specific look he wants for the first person patients see when they walk in the door." She shrugs, and I glare at her back as I follow her to the break room.

"Easy for you to say. You get to wear comfy scrubs and old lady shoes all day."

She laughs, holding the door open for me, and then makes her way to the fridge as I sit at the long table centered in the room. "They're called nursing clogs, ho. I'd say jealousy-green isn't a good color on you, but I'd be lying. It matches your gorgeous eyes. You jerk."

I flip my long, dark hair I took the time to curl this morning over my shoulder and wink at her. "But who actually pays attention to what the receptionist is wearing when you come in to have your lady bits man-handled? That's the last thing I'm worried about at the gynecologist's office."

She rolls her eyes as she comes to sit in the seat next to me. "Would you read the damn article already?"

"Ugh, fine. Geez, don't get your panties in a twist," I tell her, unlocking my phone before clicking on the link I see in our message thread.

"What panties?" she snorts, and I shake my head at her before I start to read what she sent me.

"Number neighbor?" I ask, and take a bite of my tuna sandwich as my eyes move across the screen. When I'm done, I look up at Jenika thoughtfully. "Have you done this?"

"No. I was waiting to see if one of my neighbors would message me first. But they haven't," she confesses.

"So let me get this straight. The last four digits of my phone number are 3808. So I'd message 3807 and 3809?"

"Yep." She pops the P.

I take another bite and chew while scrolling back up to read a screenshot the reporter had copied from a Twitter account.

Person 1: Hey there, Number Neighbor! Just wanted to say hi.

Person 2: Who is this? What's a Number Neighbor?

Person 1: My name is Elle. You have the next digit up from my phone number. Just a fun Twitter thing.

Person 2: I wasn't aware LOL

Person 1: Anyhoo, just checking in. Sorry to message so late. Couldn't sleep.

Person 2: haha, that's what neighbors are for. In

yo business and always at the wrong time *laughing emoji

I giggle at that, reading through a couple more screenshots of text messages between strangers. Some people get a little hostile and end up blocking the original texter, obviously lacking a sense of humor, while others end up having nice conversations.

"What do you think you'd say if one messaged you?" I ask her curiously.

She smiles wickedly. "I'd ask them if they're hot and single."

I throw my head back and laugh. "Of course you would."

She lifts one shoulder and tilts her head to the side. "I mean, why not? It's no crazier or more dangerous than meeting someone online. This would just be way more random." After a beat, she turns the question on me. "What about you?"

I purse my lips before answering. "If I hadn't read this first, I would've probably been hesitant and caught way too off guard to play along. But now, I think it'd be pretty cool. This one screenshot showed a conversation between a twenty-year-old college student and this lonely little grandma, and now they meet up for coffee every Sunday morning before church they realized they both attended."

"I guess that might be pretty common in smaller towns, since the area codes would be the same."

I nod. "But we live in big-ass Houston. There's no telling who we'd end up chatting with." I bare my teeth in a grimace, thinking of the horrible possibilities. "Yeah, I think I'll just wait and see if mine messages me first. I don't think drug dealers and gang bangers would take the time to play a fun little Twitter game. They're a little too busy with their other activities."

She taps her chin with the tip of her finger. "True story. It's probably just hipsters and people bored at work scrolling through their feeds." She seems to think for a moment. "Unless some rapist happens upon the article and gets a bright idea to text their neighbor to try to catch his next victim."

"Aaaaand you just took it there. Way to ruin a fun fantasy," I tell her, throwing my zip-lock bag into my lunch kit before pulling out my bag of pretzel chips.

"Fantasy, huh?" She grins, reaching over and stealing one of my chips.

"Well yeah! How amazing would it be if your text-door neighbor messaged you, you asked them if they were hot and single, they answered yes and sent you a selfie, and they were, in fact, hot and single? It'd be like... fate brought you together."

She laughs before standing and walking over to the sink to rinse out her leftover container. "See? I knew you'd dig it. Now we just gotta wait it out and see if our knights in shining armor just so happen to be one digit different from our own phone numbers."

She gives me a wave before returning to work while I finish up my lunch. While munching on the last few chips in the pack, I pull up my Facebook app and type out a post.

Have y'all heard of Number Neighbors or Text-Door Neighbors? Such a cute idea. If mine is out there, feel free to message me! I promise not to threaten harassment charges. Bonus points if you're a hottie. #singleandreadytotextminglewith-astrangerwhoisntamurderer

CHAPTER 2

Owen

I read her post over and over again, a smirk tugging at the corner of my lips as I sit in the dark, waiting for her to get home. I *knew* she wanted to be watched by a neighbor. Little does she know I'm her *actual* neighbor. The house next door to hers that she believes is vacant gives me a perfect view into her bedroom window.

Depending on how deep my need to be near her and watch her sleep is, I either watch her from my car sitting in the alley driveway between our houses—a different car than the one I use every day, or I do it from here, the second-floor bedroom overlooking her one-story home. It contains the only piece of furniture in the entire place—an elegant four-poster canopy bed with sheets so soft I imagine they feel like her flawless skin. I lie in that bed sometimes and envision her swaying those hips in a sultry dance for me, getting me hard and ready for her before she climbs me and takes me like a woman wild and unhinged.

Tonight, I lie in bed and wait for her to get home from her hot yoga class. I would have taken the class like I usually do, so I could watch her from the opposite side of the packed studio, but my body is worn and torn from my strenuous workout I had this morning. My feet pounded against the cement as I ran my six miles, and when I realized that wasn't going to be enough to get my rage out after what I saw her doing just a mere eight hours before I ended up on my 3:00 a.m. run, I hit the punching bags.

She was with another man. A *date*—a word I despise. Dating seems so trivial and naïve, something one does as a teenager. I've never been one to date, so the thought is humorous to me. That was until I saw my woman on a date with someone who wasn't me. Suddenly, dating seemed very serious and something I wished didn't exist.

"Fuck." I kick the sheet off me and stand. I did my best to change my train of thought today, but it was useless. Her class should have ended. Her drive is an easy eight minutes. Yeah, I fucking timed it. My woman should be at home and in bed so I can spend the night looking at her. "Naughty woman, making me wait. She'll pay for that when I finally make her mine," I say to the empty room, and like something straight out of a cheesy movie, her car pulls into the driveway.

I take the few strides from the bed to the window and watch her. She's checking her phone, laughing, and I pull mine to my face, seeing the post still up on my phone. I reread the number neighbor post and dive into the comments.

I see she just responded to Jenika's comment.

Jenika: I did it. Turns out my number neighbor is a fifty-five-year-old man with 17 cats—one aptly

named after his dead wife. #betterluckwithyourneighbor

Ivy: Mine hasn't found me yet, and I ain't as desperate as you. Guess we will have to wait. #selfcontrol #youredesperate

Jenika: Bitch

Ivy: I love it when you talk dirty to me #hopeyouremynumberneighbor #whyyousoobsessedwithme

Her humor is one of the many things I crave from her. I'm not a man of many words. Usually when I speak, it's without a trace of comedy. One of the reasons I picked her to be mine is that sassy mouth.

Just then, my phone rings and it's my closest friend, Mena. I asked him to call me when he finished work for the day, and in his line of business, that could be late.

"Mena, hey, man. Thank you for calling back so soon."

"Anytime, brother. What's up? You said you needed a favor? Tonight's not another guys' night where I beat your ass in poker and go home with all your money."

"Fuck off. It was one time and you know it was only because I felt bad that you were going broke thanks to all my winnings." I watch her with laser focus, multitasking as I pay attention to our conversation. His ball busting is not lost on me.

"Whatever. What's up?"

"Listen, I need an address for a phone number. Can you get that for me?"

He lets out a knowing scoff. "Who is she?"

I lose sight of her as she goes into the bathroom and shuts the door—something she rarely does at home, but on some occasions, she does it absentmindedly. "None of your business. I'll pay you a grand for the address."

"I'm starting to think you're only friends with me to use my line of work to chase down your conquests." He laughs. He knows I like to research the women I find interest in, but if he only knew this woman has me doing more than just a standard background check, he wouldn't give me access to something like this.

"Well, you keep nagging me like a bitch and it may just turn into that. Now get me an address for this number."

"Fine. But you owe me." Mena is a private investigator and has many resources, so this is a small page out of the book of tricks he has up his sleeve.

"Yeah, a thousand bucks," I say matter-of-factly. I rattle off the number I need him to find, and he jots it down, giving me a confirmation before we end the call.

"I got it. I will have it for you in about an hour. Poker night still on for Tuesday?" he asks.

"Yes. Really, I don't mind paying you the grand, because I'll just win it all back in the game."

"Oh, he's got jokes." Mena chuckles. "She must really have you all giddy inside if you just joked, Mr. Dark and Broody," he teases.

"Get the address and I will see you Tuesday." I don't entertain him.

"All right. Bye, man."

I end the call just as she steps out in a towel, and it has my dick instantly hard. Her chest is still damp from the shower she took. I can see the droplets glistening on her tan skin. "You are so fucking breathtaking, angel. You don't even know it." I touch the window, eager and aching to touch her.

I could go to her now, confident in my ability to claim her and make her want me. But there is something I crave about having her like this.

I'm not a crazy man.

Just a man possessed by his woman.

I'm not stalking her, per se. Just keeping her safe and watching over her before I claim what's mine. Learning everything I can about her from a distance so I'll know what she wants and needs before I approach and mark her as mine.

"Drop the towel," I murmur, and I see the reflection of my eyes crinkling in the corners when she does. I swear it takes all my restraint to not barge over there and take her with fervor. "Fuck, beautiful."

I stroke my cock, angry and fast, unable to stop.

I need her.

I have to get this going, because I can't stay away anymore.

She lies on her bed then, grabbing her glasses from the bedside table and placing them on her delicate nose. Holy shit. She's naked, her hair clinging to her neck and luscious tits, those glasses framing her gorgeous eyes, and embarrassingly I come just a minute after getting hard. It comes out ferociously, hot spurts of cum hitting the window.

"Ivy! Fuck, Ivy!" I growl, dropping my head against the frame of the window, and my breath is heavy as I come down from my orgasm.

Just then, my phone buzzes. Mena didn't even take the full hour. The address of the person I need to find is in his message.

"Times up, angel. You're mine."

The next day, I climb out of my car and head for the stairs of the shitty apartments slapped dead center in one of the roughest parts of town. Locking my Mercedes, I take two steps at a time up to the second floor.

After I bang on the door of my destination, I hear a man holler, "Damn! Just a minute." I all but roll my eyes. Little does this man know I'm about to make him an offer he can't refuse. "Why y'all be bangin' on my door?" He stops when he sees me.

I stand at 6'6", my biceps triple the size of his. He is maybe 5'8", and my presence intimidates him; I can tell by the gulp he takes. "I am an impatient man and I'm here to settle some business."

"Listen, I don't owe Jared that much. If he comin' to collect, then tell'm I'll pay'm back when I make my next drop."

I scoff arrogantly. Of course. He would be a drug dealer and owe a debt, living in a place like this. It makes this all that much more convenient. "How much is it you think you owe?" I go along with his line of thinking, letting him believe I'm here to collect.

"Two grand. I can make that within the month." He sniffs, wiping his hands on his dirty T-shirt.

I turn my head to the left, pausing to think about just how comical all this is. It couldn't be more perfect if I wrote the script. "I'm not with Jared, but I will pay you the two grand to settle your debt, all for one small exchange. If you will."

He gives me a quizzical look with his bloodshot, beady eyes. "Who the hell are you?" he questions.

"The man who is going to keep you from getting your kneecaps broken or worse. You want the deal or not? I'm running out of patience." I inhale deeply, my nostrils flaring. I don't have time for this shit. I'm a man on a mission, and I want to accomplish it immediately.

"Fine. What do you want?"

I lean in just a bit. "I just need you to change your phone number."

As if I just asked him to solve world hunger, he looks dumbfounded. "My phone number?"

"Yes. I will pay your two grand and some change for the inconvenience, all in exchange for your number."

There is a pregnant pause, and I can tell he's trying to think of all the possible reasons why I would ask such a small and absurdly random request. But like any junkie in debt, he can't say no to the cash flow. "Fine. I want all cash."

"No problem," I say with finesse.

I always get my way, and my next conquest is my Ivy.

One step closer.

Two hours later, I'm pulling up to my penthouse downtown, in need of a stiff drink and determined to get right down to business. Stepping into my sterile residence with a high-rise view, I set my keys into the glass bowl next to the door and kick off my boots. Walking to my fully stocked liquor cabinet, I grab a tumbler and fill it with aged scotch. As I round the counter and head to the white leather sofa in my living room, I get comfortable, settling in. I pick up my new phone with only one contact saved to it.

Me: Hello, Number Neighbor.

I throw back the small amount of scotch in my glass and wait, watching for a long while until the message finally says Read and those dancing dots appear across the bottom of the screen.

Her reply finally comes, and a cocky grin splays across my face.

Ivy: You have got to be kidding me

And so it begins, angel.

CHAPTER 3

Ivy

Me: You have got to be kidding me

This fad must really be getting around. I mean, anyone with a social media could have come across the Number Neighbor articles and screenshots. But what are the odds that one of the two people owning the phone numbers on either side of mine would see any of it and actually message me? Astronomical, I'm sure.

Just go with it, Ivy. You put it out in the universe, and the universe answered.

(281) 555-3809: You must not have heard of this game. A number neighbor is the person with one digit behind or ahead of your phone number. Sorry to bother you. *smile emoji

And now my poor neighbor—who already seems like a really nice person—probably thinks I'm a dick because of my response. Ugh!

Me: No! It's okay! I have. I was just super

surprised you actually messaged me. I swore I wouldn't be the first to text, in case my neighbors weren't on the up and up LOL!**

The dots indicating the person is typing dance along the screen, my excitement growing now that the initial shock has worn off. I stretch out beneath my sheets, naked as the day I was born. A year ago, you wouldn't have caught me dead in bed without a full set of pajamas on. It's all part of my self-help routine, learning to be more comfortable in my own skin. I've worked myself up to even being able to change with my curtains open. But I think that's probably only because I know the house next door is empty. An old lady lived there for a while after her husband died, but it was way too much house for her to live in on her own, so she moved away. He had already passed when I moved into mine. I see a car in the driveway every once in a while, but I figure it's either a realtor or the person assigned to keep it up coming to check on it. There was a For Sale sign in the yard for only a hot second, but no one ever moved into it.

(281) 555-3809: Smart. My name is Hunter. I'm definitely on the up and up. But if I weren't, would I really tell you? *wink emoji

I smile and sniff out a laugh as I reply.

Me: My line of thinking was that anyone too bad wouldn't take the time to play some silly Twitter game. Nice to meet you, Hunter. My name is Ivy. First—how old are you? Are you old enough to be texting this late? I'm 22.

(281) 555-3809: Haha, yes. I'm definitely of age and not jailbait. I'm 34. What do you do, Ivy?

**Me: I'm a medical office receptionist. Have to start at the bottom of the totem pole. I'm hoping to move up to become the office manager one day, maybe even the doctor's executive assistant.

Immediately, Dr. Sage's devastatingly handsome face fills my mind, and I feel almost guilty for talking to another man. Which is absolutely ridiculous. Dr. Sage barely acknowledges my existence each day when he walks in the door. It's partly the reason I'd love to move up in positions, just so I could have more interaction with him. If I were the office manager or his assistant, he'd have no choice but to speak to me more than just his curt "Good morning, Ms. Rosewood" every weekday morning.

(281) 555-3809: A young woman with aspirations. I like it. I own my own business. I didn't really like working for other people, wanted things done my way without being questioned.

My brow furrows at this, wondering what kind of business he owns. But I want to keep things light and fun, so I don't dive too deep.

Me: A control freak, are we? LOL! That's ok. I'm the opposite. I like to help make people's life easier. When all those movies showed people running around getting coffee and picking up their boss's dry cleaning, wanting to make it seem like they were miserable, it had the reverse effect for me. I was like... THAT. That's what I want to do. I like to be needed, I guess.

(281) 555-3809: I definitely am a control freak. I like order and routine. I guess I'm pretty boring.

Me: Aw, don't feel too bad about it. I bet it wasn't part of your routine to text a random number to see who would answer, am I right? *big smile emoji

**(281) 555-3809: Haha, very true. I suppose I'm

trying to better myself. Break out of my shell, you could call it.

I sit up in bed at that, the sheet falling to my lap and leaving my naked chest bare. I fight the urge to cover myself, chanting a mantra in my head. *No one can see you but you. You are beautiful. There is no one here who can hurt you. Your skin grows thicker with each moment you spend getting to know your own body and starting to love it. No one can love you until you love yourself.*

When the urge to run into my closet and put on flannel pajamas to cover every inch of my skin passes, I crisscross my legs beneath my covers, hunching over my phone to type with both thumbs.

Me: I just so happen to be going through a bit of self-betterment as well.

(281) 555-3809: Oh yeah? Not to get all nosey, but what are you working on? Could be pretty therapeutic to talk to a stranger, someone you'll probably never meet in real life. Ya know, just to vent. I guess that's sorta what I was unconsciously hoping for when I messaged my number neighbor. Talk to someone who doesn't know me already. I admittedly have a hard time meeting and getting to know other people. Which is what I'm working on myself.

I tilt my head to the side. What could be the harm? It's not like this person could find me using just my name and phone number.

You already told him you work at a doctor's office.

Yeah, but if he suddenly showed up at my work, Dr. Sage would protect me and scare him off. Right?

In your dreams.

Fuck it. For all I know, this could be fate, like Jenika

and I were talking about. This could be my knight in shining armor, my soul mate. This could be kismet.

Me: You're right. Why not? I'm working on some self-esteem issues I have. I've never been comfortable in my own skin, always worried I'm not good enough, pretty enough, that kind of thing. I guess that's why I've always wanted to be an executive assistant. I know I'm really good at helping people. My organizational skills and such are phenomenal. I can easily prove myself worthy when it comes to that. I'm great on the inside. Now I just need to learn to be happy with my outside.

And then I wait, holding my breath. It seems to take forever for him to reply. Did I scare him off with my childish insecurities? Did I sound shallow and whiny?

I breathe a sigh of relief when the dots finally reappear, realizing how much I've wanted to talk to someone without the worry of being judged.

(281) 555-3809: I mean, I can already tell you're a beautiful person on the inside. That's easy to see just in the way you crave to help people.

I smile at that, and then surprise myself by feeling giddy when I see he's typing something else.

(281) 555-3809: And well... you could always send me a picture. Then I could tell you if you have anything to worry about on the outside. *wink emoji

I snort. He's crazy. I look down at myself, seeing all my exposed skin.

Me: There's no way in hell I'm taking you a picture right now.

(281) 555-3809: *wide-eyed emoji Oh? May I ask why not? I'm not a perv... not a fuckboy asking for

nudes. Honestly just curious what you look like, since you're trying to work on your self-esteem about the way you look.

I giggle at how he has no idea I actually *am* nude.

Me: Well, I'm 5'6", 145 lbs. I have dark hair to the middle of my back that I've been curling lately, since an article I read said I'll feel more confident in my appearance if I put effort into it. I have my mom's green eyes. My dad named me Ivy, hoping that if he named me after something green I'd be more likely to inherit her color over his chocolate brown. Um… I'm still pretty tan from going to Galveston a few times this summer, but it's starting to fade. Oh, I feel like I have abnormally large teeth. I don't know if it's because they're so white or what, but people always make remarks about how big my smile is. Good enough?

(281) 555-3809: Not even close. Now you have me even more curious. I really want to see that smile. It sounds infectious. I could use a smile.

I slouch back against my pillows, reading his words over and over. What could it hurt to send the guy a picture of just my face? It wouldn't be any different than him coming across my profile on a dating site. I have all sorts of photos up on my social media accounts, many of which are public. A simple Facebook search of the name Ivy in Houston and he could easily be looking at my profile in minutes.

Clicking the photos icon in our text window, I scroll through my pictures until I find a selfie I took the other day to send to Jenika to show her the new mascara I tried out at Sephora. Before I can talk myself out of it, I send it to Hunter.

I bite my lip as I wait for his response.

(281) 555-3809: In the words of my lovely number neighbor—You have got to be kidding me.

I don't know how to take that. So all I send is...

Me: *side eye emoji

(281) 555-3809: That's you? Like... really you? You're not catfishing me right now?

Me: LOL! No. I mean, yes, that's really me. No, I'm not catfishing you.

(281) 555-3809: YOU have self-esteem issues? What in the world for? You are absolutely beautiful. I expected... I don't know. Certainly not... you.

My entire body grows warm at his words.

It makes me want to know him. Makes me want to continue talking to him. So much so, I save him to my contacts.

Me: Thank you *blushing emoji

HunterNumberNeighbor: You're more than welcome.

Me: So what about you? What do you look like?

It takes a couple minutes, which feels like forever, before he starts to reply. When the picture downloads, I all but drop my phone on my face taking it all in.

The photo shows the most gorgeous male physique from the neck down. Each shoulder is the size of my head, one leading down to an arm rippling with muscles while the other is stretched out to take the selfie. His chest could be the mold for Batman's body armor, with a dusting of dark hair. His stomach is ridged with a two... four... six... *eight*-pack, I count, with those delicious Jesus muscles I want to trace with my tongue, where they disappear into his gray sweatpants. And covering every inch of perfect flesh is an intricate maze of black-and-gray ink from his collarbones down.

Me: Holy shit.

And then I start to giggle uncontrollably.

Me: Where you goin' dressed like a slut?

I shake my head at his reply.

HunterNumberNeighbor: I'm sorry?

Me: LOL! It's a meme I saw once and almost died laughing. It said "When your boyfriend walks out in gray sweatpants and a white tee. Me: Where you goin' dressed like a slut?"

A moment passes before the dots dance.

HunterNumberNeighbor: I'm sorry. I'm lame. I still don't get it *face palm emoji

Me: It's a well-known fact that it's hot as hell when a guy wears gray sweatpants and a white tee. It affects women the same way booty shorts and a crop top with side-boob affect men, AKA dressing like a slut.

HunterNumberNeighbor: Ah *laughing emoji But I wasn't wearing a white tee.

Me: No. No you absolutely were not. That was really you?

HunterNumberNeighbor: Cross my heart.

Me: Wow. Do you work out? Hehe JK. Duh.

Me: Oh, and I totally wasn't slut-shaming. #girlpower

I go to point out I still don't technically know what he looks like, since his selfie cut off at his face, but then he distracts me with his response.

HunterNumberNeighbor: What do you mean? Are you?

Me: Am I what?

HunterNumberNeighbor: Are you a slut, Ivy?

My face grows warm at this turn in conversation.

"Ugh, what did you do, stupid girl? You were having a perfectly nice, innocent conversation, and then you had to go and steer it in a sexual direction. You brought it upon yourself," I scold myself, drawing my legs up so my knees are pointed toward the ceiling.

I decide to be honest, since I feel no need to lie to impress this guy. It's not like anything will come from this conversation. It's just all in good fun.

Me: Unfortunately, no, I'm not. I'm the opposite actually. I just don't condone slut-shaming, because I believe women should be able to sleep with whoever the hell they want without being looked down on for it.

HunterNumberNeighbor: Agreed. And what do you mean by "opposite" exactly? You don't seem like a prude, which would by definition be the opposite of a slut.

I shake my head, even though he can't see me.

Me: No, I'm not a prude either. I've just... never had sex before. A slut's number would be high. I'm the opposite of one, because my number is very, very low. Zero, to be exact.

And just like all my friends say when they find out I'm still a virgin, his next text doesn't surprise me in the slightest.

HunterNumberNeighbor: And you said you're 22?

I roll my eyes, beginning a defensive reply, but his incoming text stops my fingers.

HunterNumberNeighbor: That's impressive. I wish I would've saved myself for someone special.

I bite my lip, trying to think of how to word my response.

Me: I had more important things to worry about when I was younger. And then I had all these issues with my body and never felt comfortable letting anyone else see me, let alone touch me or even get close to me. Hell, if I couldn't stand the sight of me naked, how could I let another person see it?

Hating how heavy the conversation has gotten, I do what I always do and make a joke.

Me: And that's why I'm balls-deep in reading every self-help book/article written on the subject.

HunterNumberNeighbor: If your body is even a fraction as lovely as your face, then you have nothing to be ashamed of.

Before I can thank him for his sweet words, another message arrives.

HunterNumberNeighbor: Tell me about what some of these self-help books are saying. Don't they usually have exercises for you to try? Steps to take?

I don't know why, but I love the fact that he's asking me about that. He didn't ask me to send him a picture of my body for him to see for himself and judge. Instead, he's asking me about what I'm going through. I turn on my side, curling into a ball as I type.

Me: Well, it's actually been hard to find the right books. Most of the ones I find are for dealing with things like "loving your body after having a baby" or gaining/losing weight, or if you've been physically scarred in some way. I have no RATIONAL reason for my aversion to nudity. In my brain, I know my body is that of an average 22-year-old chick, but it

still makes me extremely anxious to not be covered up.

HunterNumberNeighbor: Gymnophobia.

Me: *side eye emoji

HunterNumberNeighbor: Gymnophobia. According to medicinenet.com, "gymnophobia is an abnormal and persistent fear of nudity. Sufferers of this phobia experience undue anxiety even though they realize their fear is irrational. They may worry about seeing others naked or being seen naked, or both. Their fear may stem from anxiety about sexuality in general, from a fear that their bodies are physically inferior, or from a fear that their nakedness leaves their bodies—and the personalities—exposed and unprotected."

Me: Sounds about right.

HunterNumberNeighbor: You didn't seem too anxious when you saw my body.

I smile at that.

Me: Only if you count the fact that I almost dropped my phone on my face... and I might've drooled a little.

Hunter: *wink emoji

Hunter: So if we cut that factor out of the definition, then that means it comes from either you being scared of sex OR you're scared of being physically and/or emotionally exposed and vulnerable. I don't think it's the physically inferior part, because you already said you know your body is "average." Although I seriously doubt there's anything average about you, lovely Ivy.

This... man. This completely wonderful stranger. He's taking the time to not only chat with me, but to look up my issues and discuss them in order to try to help me figure it all out. Who the hell does that? Even my friends don't put that much into a conversation.

Granted, I don't openly discuss my issues with my friends.

So why is it I feel so comfortable baring my soul to this guy? Airing my deepest fears to him?

CHAPTER 4

Owen

My woman suffers from gymnophobia. That beautiful goddess, with tits so luscious and full, and an ass that would have me and any man with a pulse crawling on our knees for. And that pussy. I've only seen it from outside the window, but I know if I could get between those bare lips and touch that virgin sex, that beauty would melt in my mouth.

Who made you ashamed of that breathtaking body, my sweet girl?

Ivy: If I tell you any more tonight, dear Hunter, then I would have to kill you. And judging by your physique, I'd have to think of something crafty, since I definitely don't have the strength to take you. That, and I am too lazy to do that cardio. Ya know—kill you, then I'd have to drag your body to the car, then out of the car, and then... fuck. I'd have

to dig a hole? Okay, I just realized someone could read these texts, and now my alibi is shot.

I laugh. She's witty, hilarious, adorable, fuckable, and absolutely all mine. But judging by her deflecting, I believe it's the latter. She can't be emotionally exposed and vulnerable. Ivy lacks intimacy, because she is terrified of it.

That will be the first thing I change. I'm going to teach her how to worship my body, how to sit at my feet and peer up at me while she begs to ride my cock like she was made for it. Because she was. And while she worships me, I'll praise her, eat her alive with my senses—touch, sight, and taste. Then I will come inside her as she rides out her climax on my cock, and I will tell her that her body was made to take and give pleasure for only the two of us.

I will make her realize her worth. She will have no phobia left when I get my hands on her—except for one that leaves her scared to live without me.

There is so much more to Ivy and the passion and lust I feel for her. But right now, every breath I take is to make her want me, and I'm convinced it's the very way I will be able to make her mine completely. I want to fuck her until her only vocabulary is my name and "please, more!"

I smile at her laughing at her own comment, proud of her conversation changer. I let her have it for now.

Me: You're pretty funny, so I guess the whole self-help thing is going well. You love helping people. Have a gorgeous fucking smile. And you're witty. Careful, Number Neighbor. You might just make me trip and catch some feelings.

I imagine her biting that lip, taking a second to respond before standing then walking to the full-length mirror, naked except for barely-there, lace, black panties. They'd look like they're painted onto her exquisite flesh they fit so perfectly. When I look down at my screen and see the camera symbol in place of the dancing bubbles, indicating she's taking a picture, my brow furrows. If she's doing what I think she is, my breath catches in excitement, but my rage boils.

"Don't you do it, naughty girl," I whisper into the air. My dick grows hard just thinking about it. Fuck!

I stare at my phone, waiting for her next move, praying she sends me a selfie of her glorious body, yet growing hot with anger at the same time. She doesn't know who I am, and something about the thought of her sending a naked photo to *anyone* drives me mad. Of course, it's *me*, but she doesn't know that, and I don't want her sharing her body.

I sound mental, the entire concept of my thoughts not making any rational sense. I linger on the border of two polar opposite emotions and wait as if I were standing on the edge of a cliff.

But then her self-doubt must creep in, because the camera icon disappears and is replaced with the dots. I release a breath I didn't know I was holding. I'm still not sure what side of my brain would've won, but her response takes me off that train of thought.

Ivy: Now don't go doing that. Have my messages not taught you anything? I basically laid out my plans of how I would kill you. If you fell for me, that would make you some sort of masochist. #JUSTSAYING #imnotjudging.

I give a low chuckle in my chest. But then my alarm goes off, signaling I need to get to bed so I can make my gym session with my trainer in the morning. If I keep missing them because I'm sitting outside of Ivy's house at all hours of the night, then he's going to kick my ass even harder. Which would be hellacious, because I'm already in impeccable shape.

Me: Very true, very true. Well, it's getting late and I need to get some rest. You should too, lovely Ivy. Don't dream of my 8-pack too much tonight. *wink emoji

Ivy: *eye-roll emoji Don't flatter yourself too much. Night, Number Neighbor.

Clicking the button on the side of my new phone, I put it to sleep and make my way to my bedroom. I can't wait to talk to her again.

The next morning, my 4:00 a.m. alarm goes off, and I drag my ass to the gym. My trainer and Mena are both there. Today is training day, and we plan to hit the boxing ring. I need it. I barely slept last night, too wrapped up and consumed with Ivy. The things she shared—and almost shared but didn't. I think of her taking that picture, and the idea of her sending it to some man who isn't me just doesn't sit well.

I'm bordering on insanity. So I do what I know best, since I'm pent up with rage, arousal, and tension. I hit hard, showing my trainer I'm not fucking around and he should be careful with what words he says to me today. He tends to bust my chops most days, and usually I'm okay with it. Hell, I even give it back tenfold. But not today.

When I finally did close my eyes last night, I saw Ivy in my dreams, but it wasn't the usual one—the ones with her on her knees, sucking my cock while her eyes look up at me so lovingly. No, it was her talking to someone else. I could see it was a man she was speaking to, but I couldn't quite make out his features. It was more of a shadow of him, and she was looking at him with those gorgeous eyes in a way she should only look at me.

I wanted to rip him limb from limb when he reached out and touched her back. But I couldn't. I woke up in a cold sweat sometime during the torturous dream, and it hit me then.

I'm her stalker.

There is no way she would ever fall for her stalker.

CHAPTER 5

Ivy

I wore less makeup today, something I do when I get the occasional bold pep in my step. I slept well last night, my mind still on Hunter. I can't believe it actually happened and that I opened up to him in the way I did. I mean, it's not like me to just let people in, but that's part of this whole new self-help journey I'm on. It's also nice to have new friends. So why not?

I grab myself a coffee, Jenika her usual green tea, and Dr. Sage his black cold brew.

"Jenika. Don't worry—I got it. Thanks, bitch," I remark sarcastically, greeting my favorite girl as I struggle to get in the door with my hands full. Walking into the office, I see Jenika's hair is up in a fun-styled bun, unique and very much like her. Her makeup is a brighter color today, going with the summer trends we read about on Buzzfeed between patients.

"You're welcome, hooch." She shrugs, and I roll my eyes.

I place the drinks down and then slide my bag off my shoulders before placing my glasses atop my head and plopping down in my seat.

"You're not going to believe what happened last night."

"You played DJ Clitoris to Game of Thrones."

This gains her another one of my infamous eye rolls I reserve mostly for her. "No, I save that for Judge Judy," I quip, gaining her gorgeous, lopsided smile. "Anyway, before I was so rudely interrupted." I start up my computer by shaking the mouse and then type in my password. I swivel my chair toward her and see she's waiting with a quirked brow and an "I'm waiting" look on her face. "My number neighbor texted me."

She pauses, the tip of her pen sitting between her teeth as her face remains unreadable and impassive. I can't tell what she's thinking. Then after what feels like a small eternity, she scoffs.

"Piss off. They did not." She shakes her head, turns to her computer, and continues typing in patient notes.

"I'm serious. He texted me. Hunter—that's his name—and he texted me. No bullshit, Jenika, and I swear I almost had a lapse in judgment." This earns me her partial attention.

She turns her head just slightly and squints her eyes, trying to decide whether to go along with it or if I'm pulling her leg. "Prove it. I want to see them."

I shake my head, pulling out my phone from my purse and scrolling to the very first message he sent. I won't let her scroll too much, because I can't have her seeing I divulged one of my biggest secrets to a stranger when I haven't even told her. Jenika is laid back and all about being a "let it roll off your shoulders" type, but I still think it would hurt her just a little. She's my best friend. The Grey to my Yang.

I watch her eyes as she reads it over—one, two, three exchanges down. "Well slap me on the tallywacker and call me Barbara," she remarks in a terrible attempt at a British accent.

I giggle. "That's not the saying. And now you're British?"

"Shut up, hooch, but oh my actual God. So like... did you flirt and sext?" She wiggles those brows and I flush, my gymnophobia starting to show through.

"No. I mean..." I pause then let out a huff. "You can't judge me when I tell you this!" I give her a stern look.

"I won't! Spill. It's almost time for Mrs. Peeson to make it in."

I chuckle at the nickname she gave one of our regulars, Mrs. Neeson. She has a ton of cats and always smells like their urine.

"We talked, flirted a little, but not in like, a traditional way, I guess? It was more of a passive flirtation. But... I almost sent him a nude picture, Jenika," I hiss.

Now that comment has her brows nearly flying off her head. "You dirty girl! Wait—you *almost* did? What stopped you?" She pushes on my shoulder, and I drop my head in my hands, shaking it and letting out an exasperated groan.

"Him. God, it's *him*. I can't think about showing myself to anyone that way but him." She knows who I'm talking about. I don't need to say his name.

"Oh, Ivy, you can't keep pining over him. He's so cold and dismissive at times. You know you can't cross that line." She turns off her sarcasm and her voice lowers, as if she just stepped into the den of a lioness and needs to calm her down.

"I know that, but it still just didn't feel right. I can't date or even talk to a man without seeing him in my mind. They aren't him." And as if I conjured the man in question with my thoughts, Dr. Sage walks in. He looks immaculate in a three-piece suit sans tie. It's dressy, yet he somehow makes it look casual. My breath hitches and my heart rate jacks to two hundred beats per minute. I stand on shaky legs, nearly losing my footing, but I catch myself, placing my hand on the counter.

"Good morning, Dr. Sage. I got your favorite cold brew," I tell him, my voice all breathy.

He looks me over, and I wish it were a look of desire and lust, but his expression is blank. It makes me even more aware of my insecurities and fears. I swallow past the lump in my throat as he stops and collects the coffee from my hand. Our fingers touch, and I swear I feel my leg pop like a cheesy romantic comedy.

"Thank you, Ivy. I need it. I had a late night going over some of my files. Speaking of, I would like to see Mrs. Dower's latest blood test she had done at the hospital. I saw something alarming on her ultrasound and want to follow up, but I need all the results from her hospital stay. I require them no later then 11:00 a.m., so have them on my desk."

I blink, my mouth opening and closing once from shock. That's the most words he's ever said to me all at one time before, and it's the first time he's ever given me an assignment other than my usual tasks of answering the phone, greeting guests, and checking them out after their appointment.

Before I can do anything other than nod, he makes his

way toward his office, and I watch him leave as I hold my breath. His suit is tight on his body, showing every single defined slab of muscle. Once he shuts his office door, I release my breath and my head starts spinning. I swear I can't get enough oxygen back into my brain, and I grow lightheaded.

"Take a seat and a breath. I will go fax a medical release request for Mrs. Dower. Don't even think for one second we're done talking about this." Jenika pulls me from my thoughts and leaves me at the desk. I look around, trying to rein it all back in.

This is what he does to me. He's cool and brisk toward me, but that's where my fucked up and twisted comes in.

I like it. I like the way he makes me feel. I yearn to gain his approval and lust. My phobia keeps me fearful of intimacy and many other things, so his dismissive behavior toward me is something that causes the slow burn in my stomach, that ache between my thighs, and that heart-wrenching pain in my chest that just longs for his desire, to come to life.

I almost sent a nude to a stranger—something I thought may help with my phobia of intimacy. I was testing boundaries, but I didn't want to test them with anyone other than the man I can't have. So now I sit here a mess as my nerves bundle into tight knots in my stomach and I don't know what to do.

Jenika has heard it all before, and she always tells me everything I don't want to hear. And right now, when my adrenaline and longing is still high, I want to be told what I want to hear. Something overtakes me then, and I can't stop my hands or my mind from what they're doing—forming an alliance.

Me: I'm in love with my boss, and I don't know what the hell to do about it.

I expect him to not respond. I mean, why would he? I probably seem crazy. No, I don't *seem*—I am. I have reached the point of needing to be admitted to the loony bin.

But I'm wrong. He does answer, almost immediately.

HunterNumberNeighbor: Well. This just got interesting. Tell me about it.

I take a deep breath. There is something about Hunter that makes me feel safe. Maybe he was right. Talking to a stranger may be just what I need. It's not like he can do anything with the information. And why would he? What does he have to gain? What's it to him other than just another conversation with some random person?

Me: I have these feelings, deep feelings of desire for him, and he doesn't even know I exist. Talk about a mind fuck. I just need someone to talk to. You game?

This time, he doesn't respond right away, and I worry I lost him. Jenika comes back to her desk just as Mrs. Neeson walks in. We share a knowing look, and before I place my phone in my top drawer, Hunter messages me back.

HunterNumberNeighbor: What do you like about him? What makes him so special to you?

His questions make it seem as though he's annoyed. Maybe a tad jealous?

No, it's a text, and they always come off differently than what we try to convey. One reason why I usually hate texting. However, he must be reading my mind when he sends a follow-up response.

HunterNumberNeighbor: I mean that in the nicest way possible, by the way. *smile emoji

I smirk, but I can't respond, because I hear Dr. Sage's office door open, signaling he's ready to see patients. I put my phone away and remind myself to answer Hunter at lunch.

CHAPTER 6

Owen

It's as if the second hand on my wall clock stops ticking with her words.

I'm in love with my boss.

In love? Not infatuated with or even just a crush. But in love? And she dropped this bomb with no regrets, no regard for her number neighbor's feelings or obvious interest in her. Friend-zoned with one sentence.

I have these feelings, deep feelings of desire for him, and he doesn't even know I exist.

Oh how very wrong you are, lovely Ivy. You can't walk into a room without every pair of eyes locking on you. There's not a person in this building who doesn't know you exist.

My heart thumps inside my chest, "deep feelings of desire for him" on an eternal loop inside my mind as I open my office door, sliding my phone into my pocket before glancing out into the reception area of my private practice. I watch as Ivy tries to stealthily put away her cell phone before I see, but I catch her every movement, her every breath.

God, how I want to reward her, tie her up and kiss and stroke every inch of her perfect skin. She's in love with me. Has deep feelings of desire... for *me*.

Before I do anything stupid, like walk up to her desk and profess my undying love for her, I move into Exam Room 1 for my first patient of the day.

By the time I make it back to my office to eat my meal prep for lunch, Ivy is already gone from her desk. She's probably in the break room with Jenika. If not, the only place she really likes to go for her lunch hour is the place around the corner that's an all-day breakfast restaurant.

My phone vibrated in my pocket several minutes ago, but since I was with a patient, I had to force myself not to read the text that could've only been from Ivy. All unprogrammed numbers in my new cell are blocked from notifications, so because she's the only person in my Contacts, she's the only person who would set off the ringer. I could barely concentrate on Mrs. Weaver's concerns about her test results, knowing my woman had sent me a message but I was unable to read and respond. Right now, she's probably thinking Hunter is ignoring her, mad that she is in love with someone else and jealous he no longer has a chance with her.

I close my office door and hurry around my desk to my leather rolling chair, leaning down to pull my meal prep out of the mini fridge before popping it into the microwave for two minutes. And then I tug my cell out of my pocket, finally allowing myself to read her words.

Ivy: Sorry it took me so long to respond. My boss has a strict no-cell rule. But I'm on lunch now. To answer your question... I... I don't really know how to answer, really. I SHOULDN'T be in love with him. Not just because he's my boss, but because... I don't have a good reason to. Like I said, he doesn't even know I exist. I get a clipped greeting from him every morning, and that's about it. So he's not particularly nice. He's just... IDK. I feel a pull toward him I've never felt with anyone else.

My heart pangs knowing I've made her feel invisible. But what else could I do? She's so young, so innocent. I couldn't bear the idea of openly flirting with her, and her in turn thinking I was harassing her, couldn't stand she might think I was too old or was just taking advantage of my authority. If I were to come on to her, would she believe I did it to all my female employees? I'd rather keep my distance—well, at least that she was aware of—than have her think of me as some creep. So I was short with her, and everyone else who worked in my office, so there'd be no chance of her quitting to avoid the awkwardness.

Ivy: What do I like about him? He's the most handsome man I've ever seen. But that sounds so shallow. His intelligence is astounding. His patients adore him, because they say he's so attentive and caring. I respect him so much. He's in his mid-thirties and already owns his own practice. I mean, he's just... amazing.

Before I think better of it, I jump on something she just said.

Me: "They say he's so attentive and caring." You

don't know this from personal experience? What kind of doctor is he?

Ivy: He's a gynecologist. And no. I've never actually been to a gyno before.

Me: I'm no expert, but aren't women supposed to start seeing one of those when they're like... a teenager?

Ivy: Well, if they happen to be sexually active when they're a teenager, then yes. But as I told you last night, Mr. Judgy Pants, I'm still a virgin. So I've had no reason to go.

Me: Okay, so I'm having a thought.

Ivy: Oh, God. Ok. I asked if you were game, so lay it on me.

Me: I clearly have no shot with you, since you're in love with someone else. And while I think you're absolutely stunning, smart, and funny as hell, I am not one to stand in the way of true love. If you feel a pull toward this dude that you've never felt before, then it obviously isn't just a little crush that I would be able to distract you away from with my hard-earned 8-pack LOL! So I'm gonna help you get him.

Do I feel guilty as hell for playing her this way, for keeping up the lie and not letting her know it's actually me she's speaking to about me?

Fuck yes.

Am I willing to give up this wide-open doorway of communication with the girl I've been so obsessively infatuated with for the past several months that I bought the house next to hers just so I could stalk her more easily?

Fuck no.

Because I have no doubt that when she finds out I'm her number neighbor, she'll want absolutely nothing to do with me. Not only that, she'll probably hate me for tricking her this way.

But it's too late now. I'm in too deep. I just want a taste of her. Just... one taste. And then I'll tell her the truth.

For now though, I've got the perfect plan.

Ivy: Wow. Like... wow, Hunter. You are as genuinely sweet as your 8-pack is glorious. *big smile emoji So how are you going to help me get him? Especially when I can barely speak when he's around. OMG. Speaking of! He gave me an assignment today! I felt like such a big deal! I know that sounds so stupid, but HE asked ME to do something for him. And I did it. And I didn't fuck it up. So maybe now he'll see he can ask me to do more for him, and he'll continue to until we're actually exchanging full sentences with each other. *wide-eye emoji

I glance at the tray on the edge of my desk and grab the file folder out of it. Sure enough, she did exactly as I'd asked. Actually, she went above and beyond what I required, going so far as to highlight Mrs. Dower's phone number so I could easily find it to call her, and she put a sticky note on one of the pages. Her neat handwriting makes me smile, seeing she labeled the blood test results for me so I wouldn't have to search through the week's worth of notes from the woman's hospital stay.

She's fucking perfect.

Me: Ok, now trust me on this. You're going to want to say no. With your gymnophobia, you're probably going to want to block me for even suggesting this, but like I said, just go with it.

Ivy: Oh, God. I'm telling you right now, if you're suggesting I just waltz into my boss's office, strip

off all my clothes, and pounce on him, you're certifiable and absolutely no help, because that would NE-VER HA-PPEN.

Me: Nope, not what I was going to say.

Ivy: All right then. Bring it.

Me: Lovely Ivy, it's about time you make an appointment to see a gynecologist. Oh look, how convenient! You happen to work for one.

Ivy: WTF?! No way! I can barely speak to the man. You expect me to be able to drop trou and let him examine me??!!

Me: Did I not warn you that you'd want to say no and just to trust me on this? Think about it, Ivy. He's "attentive and caring" with his patients. You'd get to see a whole new side of him. Plus, you'd get his hands on your pussy, which is like... the whole point, right? What easier way than to schedule it into his appointment calendar? LOL!

Outside my door, I hear her burst out laughing at her desk, so I'm not worried when I receive her next message.

Ivy: I hate you.

Me: Oh, is it opposite day? Man, I haven't played that since I was a kid. *wink emoji But for real. Are any of your coworkers also his patients?

I obviously know the answer before she sends it, but her explanation makes my chest feel full.

Ivy: Yes. All of my female coworkers are his patients. At first, I thought it was because all of them think he's deliciously gorgeous like I do. But come to find out, it's because he's really a damn good doctor and they don't trust anyone else.

To hear she thinks so highly of me makes me long for her in a way I've never felt before.

Me: So there's your opening. No pun intended. Make an appointment. He'll have no choice but to talk to you then.

Her little growl of annoyance from the reception area makes me grin, especially when I receive her short reply.

Ivy: Fine.

CHAPTER 7

Ivy

My palms are sweating and my fingers feel numb and stiff as I put my name down for his 6:00 p.m. appointment. His last one for the day. Usually, I leave at 5:30 after we check in the final patient. Well today, I'm that final patient, and it's going to be just him and me in that room.

I feel the distinct sensation of nausea rising in my stomach. I can't believe I let Hunter—who, I might add, is still very much a stranger—talk me into this. I oddly feel completely safe with him. It's as if I can be candid and unafraid when I'm talking to him. Not only that, but this whole number neighbor game has just risen to a whole new level, and the playing field has grown far too scary for someone too afraid to play. So I've gotta pull up my big girl panties and be brave.

I won't back down. Something in me fights those voices of my phobia and anxiety. Besides, he sees hundreds of vaginas a month. Mine is nothing special.

I click Save on the appointment setter screen and swallow back the rising bile.

"Shit," I whisper, seeing it is too late now. The appointment has been locked and he has been notified. I stand and start to pace, going to the printer and grabbing medical records, clumsily bringing them back to my desk. I can't breathe. The room feels small and I feel giant in it.

HunterNumberNeighbor: So? Do you have a date with the doctor or what?

His message distracts me, causing a nervous smile to spread on my cheeks.

Me: Yes. I regret it. Wish me luck.

HunterNumberNeighbor: You will do great. I know it.

Me: Yes, spread eagle in front of my boss—who I so badly want to bend me over one of his exam tables to make love to me—while he stares at my crotch. That won't be awkward at all.

HunterNumberNeighbor: I told you, lovely Ivy. If I were him, I would take full advantage of that beautiful gift you are literally putting in front of him. What if he comes on to you? Do you want that?

I gulp. The reality? Yes. God, I want him so badly, and maybe I think I would want him to come on to me, because I know it won't happen. So the fantasy is something I can relish in without so much fear.

Me: I want him to do whatever he wants to me. Haven't you ever felt that way about a woman before? You just want to ravish her in the most animalistic way. Possess her, because she wants it?

HunterNumberNeighbor: You have no idea. I've been there. The lust is kinetic. You feel this pull of

gravity and you think even being inside them isn't close enough. I have been there before.

His words are hot and stoke the lust I'm feeling. Hunter has a sensual way about him, and if I weren't so caught up on my boss, I probably would have tried something with him. Most likely a phone fling, because I wouldn't have the balls to do anything else. But he is charming and arousing through our messages.

Me: I wish he would see me like that. Maybe this was a bad idea. I'll just be another patient, Hunter. What is this even going to do? It'll just make it even more awkward when he's so curt with me. This won't get his attention.

HunterNumberNeighbor: Well, care to wage a bet? If you go in there, spread open that beautiful body to him, and something doesn't ignite in him, then he's a damn fool. And I'm always willing to be here as your back up. *wink emoji

HunterNumberNeighbor: I'll put $50 on it.

I blush, rolling my eyes.

Me: Such a dude. *eye-roll emoji

HunterNumberNeighbor: Good luck, lovely Ivy. Talk to you very soon. Can't wait to be $50 richer.

I put my phone away and bide my time, the minutes going in slow motion, feeling like hours all on their own. God. What am I doing?

I pace the room, standing in the paper robe Dr. Sage has his patients wear. My panties are still on, because I can't seem to fully commit. I tried to talk myself out of this. Jenika left twenty minutes ago, and fuck if she didn't give me all kinds of shit today for setting myself an appointment.

I'm playing with fire.

He's your boss!

I let a small sound rush out of my mouth. Rushing toward the chair to grab my clothes to back out, I'm stopped by a rap on the door. It's too late to change my mind.

"Ivy? Can I come in?"

He's here, and I'm already aching in my core, the sound of his voice causing a pool of arousal to collect at my center. I hurry and climb on the table, sitting flat on my ass and doing my best to cover myself up.

"Uh... um, yeah!" I holler, my voice shaking. Great. Just great.

He walks in and looks me over once, glancing down at my new patient paperwork just a split second later. It gives me time to look at him in the way I really like to. He's tall, 6'2", with slabs of muscles not even close to being hidden behind his navy slacks, white button-up, and emerald green tie. His shiny brown oxfords are large, showing the substantial size of his manly feet. He's breathtaking and exotic.

"How are you feeling today?" He sets my chart down and sits on the round, backless rolling chair, moving across the room until he's inches from me. His eyes dart to mine and my throat goes dry as if it were the damn Sahara Desert.

"Um, okay. I just needed a checkup?" It comes out unsure, and I all but face palm myself right there.

"A checkup. Is that a question or statement?" He smiles, a soft laugh tumbling from his beautiful lips. He's never smiled or laughed in front of me like that before.

Must be that bedside manner and patient charm they are always boasting about.

"Yeah, sorry. I'm just nervous. This is my first appointment, and you're my boss. This is all just... odd."

His eyes flash, looking me over again. He looks stoic, and sexy, and oh so fuckable.

I can't do this!

"I'm not your boss in here, Ivy. Not even close."

My breath catches. What was that? Did he mean something by that or am I just so oversensitive and aroused that I'm reading too much into it?

"Oh. Okay." He looks at me for a brief moment, and I squirm under his gaze.

"I have to ask you a few questions. Please answer them to the best of your knowledge." He turns and grabs his tablet off the table with my chart.

"Last menstrual cycle?"

My cheeks heat already. "Two weeks ago. My last day was the 9th."

He nods, entering in the information. "Are you on any medications? Birth control? Health management? Any type of therapy?"

I tuck my hair behind my ear and gear up, my hands playing with one another in my lap. "Just Xanax for anxiety on rare occasions."

He peers up, tilting his head and gaging me. "Specific causes of anxiety?"

I nod, knowing where this is going. "I have gymnophobia."

He bites his bottom lip then and look at my hands in my lap. That has me squirming in my seat. That lip needs to be between *my* teeth.

"Birth control?"

He doesn't address my phobia further and I am thankful. I'm not here to talk about that. In fact, I'm here to get over it.

"No. I would like to be though. I don't really know my options."

Setting the tablet down, he rolls back over to me, placing his hands on my knees, and I do shiver this time.

"Okay, we can talk about those options today. Let's get to the pelvic exam first." He caresses my knees with his thumbs, and if I weren't so sure I'm reading into everything too much, I'd swear he's teasing me, arousing me on purpose—claiming me.

"Are you sexually active?"

"No," I whisper.

"You planning to become sexually active?"

I swallow deeply.

"Uh... I don't... I don't know." It comes out almost as a moan, and then his eyes come up to mine. Something sparks between us, electricity igniting his touch and jolting through me.

"Lie back."

I do what he says without batting a lash. I watch as his eyes flash, and I'm hypnotized by it. I try to tell myself to be calm and stop making this all up in my head, but he holds my gaze and makes it impossible. This isn't real—

Oh my God.

As I stop dead in the middle of that thought, he does something that isn't supposed to happen, and I *know* I'm not reading into something innocent. I whimper. Dazed, confused, turned on, and a ball of mixed emotions from both ends of the spectrum.

Dr. Sage takes one of my ankles and places it on his shoulder, nipping at the skin of my calf before taking the other and putting it on his other shoulder. His eyes never leaving mine as I whimper, my chest rising and falling rapidly, as my heart races a mile a second.

"One last question, and it's a very important one."

All I can do is nod frantically and wait for him to ask.

The blue of his eyes grow darker, and I watch, mesmerized, as his expression goes from pleasant and open to possessive and animalistic. "Would you like me to eat your beautiful cunt today, Ivy?"

I choke then, the room spinning as it nearly goes black.

Owen

Her whimper sets me off, her scent overtaking my every breath as that fucking black lace between her legs grows damp just inches from my face. I didn't hold back and waste time, and I don't plan to. She wants me. If her body didn't tell me that alone, her words to "Hunter" did. I have my fuel and intel. I don't and will not wait anymore.

"Answer me, Ivy. Do you want my mouth on this breathtaking cunt?" I growl, kissing the inside of her thigh. She grips the exam table and breathes out. My cock nearly rips through my designer slacks. Fuck, she is beautiful, and she's finally mine. I've ached, longed, and lusted over her for so long, and her perfect body is splayed out for me to fucking own.

"I... I... I can't say it," she stutters, taking hold of the paper gown and crisscrossing the two edges tightly over her front.

"Say it or I will stop, and baby, this pussy needs me. It's greedy and begging, and I need to give you what you need. Say it." I use one finger to pull her panties to the side, the act raw and painfully visceral. She shaved, leaving just a strip of hair above her lips.

Fuck, that's mine.

"I want you, Dr. Sage."

I let out a relieved breath.

"Call me, Owen. Moan my name, Ivy. Fucking scream it." With that, I end the torture for us both and lean in, opening her lips and licking her from taint to clit in one long swoop.

Her taste leaves the tip of my cock wet with my excitement. It's exotic, her flavor unique. It's something I want more than the next breath I take. I reach up, bunching the material of her flimsy robe in my hands at the center of her stomach, and rip it away. This has her back arching, and her hands go straight to her full, heavy tits. Goddamn, they are even more glorious this close up.

"Don't you dare cover that body. I will tie you down if you keep that up," I growl.

"Oh my God. Owen!" she cries as I cover her pussy with my mouth once more.

I demand more of her. I crave her sounds, her screams, her filthy words that are only for me.

"You have pranced around this office in those fuck me heels and glasses for months now and caused me to come every night in a violent rage, because I can't take you." I stand then, my thumb taking the place of my tongue on her clit, as I lean over her and grab a handful of luscious breast that now belongs to me.

She squeezes her eyes shut, her phobia still ever present but losing footing the more I drown her with my relentless and insatiable need for her. With time, I plan to take all those fears and crush them with my desire for her.

"Open those beautiful eyes, baby. I need to see you. Connect with me. I fucking need you." I watch her as I lick, bite, and suck on her porcelain skin. She is fighting her mind with as much power as she can muster, and I wait for her to be strong enough to give in.

"For me. If you want me the way I know you do, then look me in the eyes and show your man who owns this cunt." I circle her clit faster with my thumb and her eyes fly open, her core tightening, an orgasm building.

But before she falls over that precarious edge, she flies up, and I lose contact with her clit.

"I want to please you," she breathes heavily, and I know exactly what she's doing, but I can't push her past it the way I have been as Hunter.

She can't know I'm Hunter. Not yet.

"Baby," I growl, fisting her hair in my hands and tilting her head to her side so I can nip at her elegant neck.

"Owen. What is happening? You—you've always been so cold to me. You acted like I was just a body at your front desk."

I lick her where her shoulder and neck meet and then bite down hard, marking her like a man possessed.

"You see why? Look how fucking crazy you make me. If I were anything other than cold, then you would have been laid out on the desk and fucked in front of everyone. I can't resist you, Ivy. I've wanted you to be mine since the moment I saw you. I always had the intention to claim and own you, but I needed the perfect opportunity."

She gasps, wrapping her legs around me and pulling me in. She knows nothing about sex, but her body knows I'm hers and she is mine, because it takes over and clings to me, her sex rubbing against my slacks-covered cock. I look down at her core rubbing against me, and the animal in me roars to life.

"Fuck yes. Just like that, baby. Circle those hips; get that clit nice and ready for me."

She cries out, lust and euphoria overtaking her body. Ivy doesn't know how to handle everything she's feeling, and that both fuels me on and has me so fucked in the head. I don't want her to think about or feel anything but me.

"You're making a mess with all those juices on my pants, baby. What are you going to do about that?"

Her innocent eyes look up at me, lust glazing them. "Take them off. I want…" She cries out when I thrust and hit her clit hard. "Ah! I want to rub myself against your cock."

Fuck me. She wants to experience me as if I was her first everything.

"You want to use my cock like it's your fingers, baby? You want to get your scent all over me? You know how hard it's going to be to not slide into that perfect, tight, wet cunt?"

She bites her lip and nods.

I sit back on my stool and put my hands behind my head. "If you want it, baby, then come and get it." I watch the trepidation slip from her face and all her lust-filled fantasies she's had for me come to a full boil.

"Yes, Dr. Sage."

"Fuck."

CHAPTER 8

Ivy

I have no idea what I'm doing. It's like I'm having an out-of-body experience as I watch myself slide down off the end of the examination table and down onto my knees in front of Owen's spread thighs. Wanting to please him, I shrug the paper gown off my shoulders, and I'm rewarded with his sharp intake of air. It fuels my confidence, and I reach for his leather belt.

With shaking fingers, I undo it, the button, and his fly, and he lifts up a little when I tug at the waistband so I can pull his dress pants and boxer briefs down enough that it frees his massive erection. My eyes flare at the sight of him. He's huge and perfect. It's the most beautiful cock I've ever seen. It may be the only one I've ever seen in person, but I've seen plenty in pictures and videos.

I tell myself to just pretend to know what I'm doing, letting my body run purely on instinct, and my instincts are telling me to put that beautiful cock in my mouth, so that's exactly what I do. I wrap my small hand around it, absently noting how my fingers don't meet my thumb, and lower my head until I can lick the precum that's escaped the slit in the tip.

His groan above me sends a shiver through me, and as his hands bury into my hair, his long, nimble fingers begin massaging my scalp instead of pushing me down as I expected. It sends prickles of pleasure down my neck, over my shoulders, until my nipples harden between us, and I finally take him into my mouth. I feel the corners of my lips stretch almost painfully in order to accommodate his girth, and it sends a rush of wetness to my already drenched pussy.

I had been seconds away from orgasming when he was rubbing my clit. The feeling that had built to an alarming intensity inside me scared me so badly I had to stop him, fearing I would explode and die from the power of it. So I stopped it. I stopped him. And in order to distract him from my worry, I turned everything on him, wanting to give him the pleasure he had given me. But there was no way I'd let him pull away before I finished him off. This might be the only opportunity I ever have to show Dr. Sage... Owen... how much I long for him.

I put everything I have into making him feel good. And for it being the first blowjob I've ever given, I can't help but feel I'm doing a damn good job, if the guttural noises and his panting breaths are anything to go by. He continues to massage my scalp as I bob on his cock, my grip moving up and down his length as my mouth focuses on his bulbous head. He's so huge I can't get him very far into me, and I gag as he thrusts his hips up and hits the back of my throat. My eyes water as I look up at him to make sure I haven't disappointed him at what I think is a failure to take him deep enough, but the pure ecstasy I see written all over his face shows me just how wrong I am.

I'd do anything to keep that look on his face, so I gag myself on his cock on purpose, and watch in pure bliss as he shudders at the sound and the feel of my throat's involuntary squeeze around him. I do it over and over again, getting more comfortable with the feeling, and with my hand jacking him, I feel his hands tighten in my hair. When I groan around his cock at the pleasurable pain he's causing me, he warns in a gust of breath, "You're gonna make me come down your throat, lovely Ivy."

I have just enough time to find it interesting he too called me what Hunter does in our conversations, when suddenly his hot cum spurts out of him and down my throat as I swallow quickly to keep up with each gush. He pulses in my fist, and his hands hold me to him gently.

When his body goes lax, he almost falls backward off his rolling stool, and I make an "Eep!" sound before grabbing his tie and pulling him forward. We both laugh as his forehead comes to rest against mine, and I watch his insanely gorgeous eyes twinkle like I've never seen before. He's unrecognizable as the broody, cold man I work for every day. Instead, he looks at me in a way my innocent, untrained mind can only identify as love. I know that's completely ridiculous, even after he confessed he's wanted me for as long as I've wanted him, so I just let the look fill me with the most confidence I've ever felt in my life.

For the first time, I'm nearly naked in front of someone, and I have not one bit of my phobia showing its ugly face. Instead, I feel pretty damn good about myself, like I could take over the world.

Wrong, Ivy. You already took over the world. And right now, he's staring at you like you're a goddess he's never letting go.

Owen

She makes me weak, something no other woman in the universe has ever been able to do. Within just moments, not only did I slip up and call her the nickname I've given her while messaging her as Hunter, but I also nearly fell out of my seat after she made me come.

Those are two things a man like me would definitely not normally do. I'm usually so controlled, so precise and careful. I'll have to watch myself more closely when I'm around her. At least until I can find a way to come clean without losing her. Because that is not an option any longer. Not now that I've had a taste of her. Not now that I've felt her delicate fingers on my flesh. And certainly not now that I've watched with my own two eyes as she went from nervous and shaking to confident and strong just by wanting to please me, and just by my praise.

No, I can't lose my lovely Ivy. I'll watch as she spreads her vines and clings to me, waiting for the opportune moment when I know she'll forgive me and can't live without me. Then I'll tell her the truth.

CHAPTER 9

Ivy

When I get home, I strip out of my clothes and make my way into my bathroom, ready to take a bath like I always do after work. But then I catch a glimpse in the mirror, and I see the marks Owen left on my skin. As my fingers trail over the bites and hickeys he left from my neck to my inner thighs, a smile pulls at my lips. I don't want to take a bath and remove his scent from my flesh. All those marks show the exact spots his mouth was on my body, leaving faint traces of his DNA. My hair smells like his cologne. I keep getting whiffs of it when I turn my head. He owns me now, and he doesn't even know it.

Just when I dip my fingers between my still swollen pussy lips to feel where his had circled my clit, my phone blares with my text tone from my purse on the bathroom counter, making me jump.

My face is hot as I scramble through the bag before

finally finding my cell, feeling like I was caught doing something dirty.

HunterNumberNeighbor: Well? The suspense is killing me. How'd it go?

Me: OMG.

HunterNumberNeighbor: *wide-eyed emoji

Me: OMGOMGOMGOMG!

HunterNumberNeighbor: *wide-eyed emoji *red double-exclamation point emoji

Me: LOL! Sooo... how much detail are you wanting here, because holy shit.

HunterNumberNeighbor: I want ALL the details.

Me: FML. Ok. So, it started out how I guess all his appointments would. He asked me a bunch of embarrassing questions, and IDK what I might've said to give him the all-clear, but next thing I knew, he was...

HunterNumberNeighbor: HE WAS WHAT??

Me: OMG I can't believe I'm telling you this. I can't even believe it actually happened.

HunterNumberNeighbor: Ivy. Tell me.

Me: Uuuugh, ok. Next thing I knew, he was... eating me out. Like, right there on the examination table. I mean, he made me tell him I wanted it first, and you'd be so proud. I DID IT!

HunterNumberNeighbor: Fuuuuuck. Then what happened?

Me: Well, within minutes, I almost had an orgasm. Well, at least I think so. From what I've read in books and watched in naughty videos, I assume that's what that feeling was. And it scared the shit out of me, so I stopped him. Guess that's why the French call it la petite mort—the little death—because it certainly felt like I might die if I let it happen.

There's a long pause, and then he finally responds.

HunterNumberNeighbor: Are you trying to tell me you've never had an orgasm before?

Me: I told you I'm a virgin.

HunterNumberNeighbor: Yeah, but like... you've never made yourself come before?

Me: Hunter *glare emoji Before a couple months ago, I couldn't even stand to be naked. Do you really think I'd be able to... touch myself down there?

HunterNumberNeighbor: Oh, lovely Ivy. We need to fix that. STAT. How will you be able to let go and let him take over your body the way you deserve, if you get scared every time he gets close to getting you off?

Me: LOL and how do you suppose we fix that, huh? *raised eyebrow emoji

HunterNumberNeighbor: We should sext, obviously.

Me: What? LMAO!

HunterNumberNeighbor: Let me walk you through it. Let me tell you what to do to yourself, and you just trust me. Look what happened when you trusted me about the appointment thing.

Me: Are you being serious right now?

HunterNumberNeighbor: Dead serious.

I glance up in the mirror at my nakedness, for once finding it beautiful now that it's decorated with Owen's marks all over it. Could I possibly go a step further and masturbate? I mean, Hunter has a point. If this continues between Owen and me, how long could I possibly keep distracting him away from me not letting him bring me to orgasm?

I must take too long thinking it over, because Hunter sends me a message changing the subject.

HunterNumberNeighbor: We'll come back to that. What happened after you stopped him?

Me: Get this: I gave my first blowjob. And I ROCKED it. Made him come. In my mouth. *hair-flip emoji

HunterNumberNeighbor: I just groaned. Out loud. Not gonna lie, lovely Ivy. I'm hard as a rock right now just reading your words.

Me: Really? I... I don't know what to say.

I can't lie to myself. Knowing I've made Hunter hard by making him think of me giving a blowjob does miraculous things to my self-confidence. I feel a little guilty talking about this with another man, but I'll never meet him in person. And it's not like Owen and I are official and exclusive or anything. For all I know, he could be fucking someone else right now.

The thought makes my heart seize in my chest.

And then it hits me.

If I want Owen to be mine, I'm going to need to get over my shit and allow him to claim me in every way. In order to do that, I won't be able to clam up every time he gets me close to coming. I'm going to have to let him see me fully. Naked. Even if the thought of him looking at my face and seeing it contort the way those women's in pornos do makes me want to vomit. I gotta lock him down.

HunterNumberNeighbor: All you have to do is exactly what I say and answer when I ask you to.

I take a deep breath, staring at the words and teetering on the edge of guilt and desire. I'm still so wound up from my moment with Owen, and I feel like I belong to him now. Like I'm his.

I *am* his—at least, that's what I believe after what we shared. We couldn't talk about what this meant for us, because the cleaning staff came through and found a leak in the patient bathroom, which demanded Owen's attention. He said he would call me later, and now I wish he would.

Me: Hunter, what about Owen? I love him. You know this.

HunterNumberNeighbor: You and I will never meet. This is purely for him. You want to give him everything, right? Show him just how fucking incredible you are. You want this right now. Don't lie, lovely Ivy.

Swallowing thickly, I close my eyes and release three breaths. I count them out, relying on them to pull me through this. If I'm going to be Owen's wildest dreams, his own goddess of desire, then I need to be Hunter's experiment.

Me: What do I do?

HunterNumberNeighbor: Fuck. Good girl.

Me: I want to be HIS good girl. Teach me how to come, please.

HunterNumberNeighbor: Lie on your back, take only your bottoms off, and leave your top on. This is going to be fast and fucking dirty.

He doesn't know I'm already naked. My clit throbs, growing slick with desire, and the image being fucked by Owen with nothing but my shirt on because he couldn't wait to get me naked has me practically panting. I go into my bedroom and climb onto the bed.

Me: Okay.

HunterNumberNeighbor: My dick is aching it's so hard for your beautiful pussy. I want you to think of his huge cock sliding against your clit. Using it as your own toy. Touch your clit, Ivy. Now.

Hunter's demand is via text message, but I swear I hear it as if he were right in front of me. But I only see Owen in my mind. I imagine it's Owen messaging me tonight.

HunterNumberNeighbor: How does it feel?

I use talk-to-text to reply.

Me: So wet.

I circle my clit and my back leaves the bed, a loud moan singing out through the thick air. I remember Owen's tongue there. It was so slick and demanding, his strokes possessive and dominating me in a way I never thought I would like. But the idea of being held down and fucked so hard like his tongue was doing has my fingers rubbing hard, fast circles.

HunterNumberNeighbor: Tell me what you did to him, Ivy.

Me: I dropped to my knees and put his huge cock in my mouth, and I sucked him so good. The way he came in my mouth... God, I loved it. I loved sucking cock. Am I bad for that?

I use one finger and try exploring, sticking my finger inside to attempt to mimic Owen's tongue when he thrust it inside me, but it's not the same.

HunterNumberNeighbor: Fuck. I've never been so hard. Do you like dirty talk, Ivy? Is it something you want to try with me to see if you like it?

I bite my lip, turning my attention back to my clit.

Me: Try?

HunterNumberNeighbor: When you were on your knees, I bet he rammed into your mouth,

because you were so hungry for it. You liked sucking cock. I want your hot mouth wrapped around me. I'm thinking about it right now.

Me: Oh wow, more.

It does turn me on, so much so that I feel heat pooling deep in my lower stomach, and my core becomes drenched with need.

HunterNumberNeighbor: Was he big? Did he fuck your mouth good?

Me: Yes. He did. He was so big I barely fit him. And he made these noises, God! It was so hot.

HunterNumberNeighbor: Yeah, because you have a hot, slutty mouth made just for it. Don't you?

Me: Yes. I loved pleasing him.

HunterNumberNeighbor: I bet you did. You probably choked on that cock while you looked up at him, didn't you, lovely Ivy? Slap your clit and then plunge two fingers in. Do it now, and tell me what you feel.

I hesitate for a minute, worried it may hurt and a little afraid of his request.

HunterNumberNeighbor: Don't make me ask twice. Slap that little clit and slam in your fingers. I want you to come with me. I'm so hard for you. So fucking hard, Ivy.

I bite harder on my lip and do as he says. I pull my hand back and then bringing it down in one swift motion. I hear the sound and feel the sensation rock me to my core as it reverberates, coursing through me.

HunterNumberNeighbor: Let go and come for me, Ivy. Fucking come. Shit. I'm coming all over you. Thinking about coming all over those tits.

I ram in the two fingers and feel myself on the brink,

but I can't get there. I. Just. Can't. Something won't let me, and I know it's not just my phobia. It's my....

Fuck! I can't come, and I growl out into the room in frustration. I pull my fingers out and slap myself again, wanting to orgasm while thinking of Hunter coming for me. I plunge the two fingers in and work my thumb on my clit, bowing my back off the bed, wanting and needing it, when something happens. My whole body seizes when I read the text.

Dr. Sage: I want you so badly, baby. I'm stroking myself while I think of that beautiful, delicious pussy. Are you thinking of me?

And just like that, it hits. Like a volcano erupting, I explode. My first orgasm floods through me, my entire body igniting in goose bumps and catching fire. Sweat beads along my forehead, and I stare at the text from Owen. He messaged me, and it set me off. I was needing *him*. That's what was missing!

I scream out, my spine nearly snapping in half as I drop the phone and cry out Owens name. "Owen! Oh my God!" Just then, my phone rings, and I see his name.

"Owen?" I answer breathlessly.

"Fuck, Ivy. I'm coming. I need you. Where are you? I need to see you." He groans like he did when he was unleashing his come down my throat.

"I'm home. My address is—"

"I know where you live. Employee records. Leave the bedroom window unlocked and a light on so I can find you. I want to come in through your window like a thief in the night and feed on you till you can't remember your own name."

I gasp, the aftershocks of my orgasm hitting me. "Owen, I... I—"

"Do not deny me what's mine. Leave the window unlocked and remove all your clothes. I want you." I gulp, my desire roaring back to life.

"Yes, sir," I reply out of habit from work.

"Ah, that's my good girl."

I whimper, hearing exactly what I've been longing for. "Owen, hurry."

CHAPTER 10

Owen

She came for me. Only when *my* text came through did she let go. I watched her outside her window as she followed "Hunter's" lead, but he couldn't get her off, because to her, it wasn't me. The second I sent her a message, giving her what I knew she needed, she came. Ivy needs me. She wants me, and the jealous beast inside me is still not tamed. I am Hunter and he is me, but she doesn't know that.

After what we shared, my jealousy runs thick in my veins over her talking to Hunter the way she did. I'm a prick, I know, for not telling her the truth, but she's not ready for it yet. I need to get inside her first and make sure she's ready for everything it means to be with a man like me. I will not just have Ivy; I will fucking claim, possess, and own her as mine. All mine.

I wait fifteen long, excruciating minutes in my car outside her house as I wait until I go in to be with her. I watch her lie on the bed, naked and sated, her hands lying on her pillow where her head is atop them. She's breathtakingly exquisite, and I need to get inside her house and inside that body. Not just physically, but emotionally and mentally. She's making me crazy in my obsession for her. Fuck.

The second the fifteen-minute mark passes, I get out of my Audi and walk right up to her window. Once I am close enough, she sees me. Sitting up, her dark hair cascades around her. Her fuck-me eyes look ravenous yet innocent all at once, and I realize this right here is my fantasy come true.

I open her window and slowly climb in. She sits still, taking me in as I tower over her and just stare down.

"Am I dressed the way you wanted?" She blushes, looking down at her body shamefully. She doesn't recognize she's doing it, but it makes me growl.

"You are so fucking perfect and beautiful. Don't look at your body in shame. It was made to be worshipped not despised."

Her eyes look up at me, searching mine. "I hate it. It makes me feel powerless."

I move then, climbing on the bed to be at her fucking beck and call. I start at the foot of her bed, grabbing her foot and bringing her ankle to my lips, leaving open-mouthed kisses. "You have gymnophobia. Where did that come from, Ivy? Did someone tell you that your nakedness is shameful?" I kiss up her calves, leaving little bites as I go, each one making her shiver.

"Yes." I can feel her body tensing on me as I kiss her right on her beautiful center. "Owen!" she cries, her hands finding my hair, trying to push me away.

She's vulnerable, because she's in her own place, her

environment. Today in the office, she was more open to her naked body and her pleasure, because she was in my space and could pretend she was someone else, someone strong and without fear. But she also stopped me from making her come, which I'm not okay with. But I respect her too much to force her beyond her limits. I have to help her, teach her—guide her.

"Who told you to be ashamed?" I ask, now kissing each of her perky nipples.

"My mother. She always said our bodies were used to sin and we should be ashamed."

Ah—there is it. "Why would she do that? Lie back, Ivy." I help her move, her eyes going wide.

"My father cheated... a lot, and my mother said he couldn't resist the sins of the flesh. She made me believe my body could ruin people."

"No. Your father was a coward for not just leaving if he was unhappy," I tell her, gripping her chin in my hand and bringing her eyes to mine. "Are you close with him?"

She shakes her head, tears coming to her eyes. "He died years ago, but when my parents got divorced, he left to be with his mistress, leaving us behind."

I kiss her cheek. How can anyone willingly walk out of her life? Ivy is wise, beyond caring, intelligent, witty, and unique. I've learned by watching and listening to her from the sidelines for a long while, studying who she is. "Are you and your mother close?" Her eyes turn dark, the saddest I've ever seen her.

"No." She's curt and her eyes drift to the window.

"Ivy, talk to me. I want to know. I want to be there for you." I bring her attention back to me.

"She was awful. She used to shave my head and make me wear layers and layers of clothes, even in the dead of summer. I was teased a lot for it. I even got sick at times. Heat stroke."

I hiss, my hand that's on the bed grips the sheet, and I hurry and move it to touch her hip so I can feel her. I need to calm down. "When did you get away?" I kiss her temple before I move us abruptly, me against her headboard and her straddling me, completely fucking naked and breathtaking. She covers herself, crossing her arms over her breasts. "You don't know what it does to me when you cover yourself like that." I change the subject for a brief moment.

"I don't. I'm sorry. I don't mean to."

"You are so beautiful. You take my breath away. Feel that? You do that to me." I grab her hips and take note at how rounded they are in my large hands. She's all woman and I'm all man. I rock her hips back and forth, her cunt gliding against my shaft in my slacks. Ivy cries out, her hands instinctively going to my chest. Her large, luscious yet perky breasts become exposed, and I hiss as we keep her moving against my length. "Your body is a work of art. These tits. God. Mine." I use one hand to cup her left breast, squeezing and gripping it.

"Ah!" she moans.

"I don't like when you hide it."

"But then you lust over me and do crazy things because of me. You sin because of me," she whispers, and my other hand goes to cup her jaw.

"What's wrong with lusting and sinning over something that belongs to me? And the only sin I plan on making is fucking you out of wedlock, which will not be for long. I don't and will never look at other women the way I do you. Do I do that to you too, Ivy?"

Her eyes widen, her breath catching at what my words

imply, and she nods. "Owen, I have wanted you since the day you interviewed me." There is a sheepish smile on her face.

"That's how it should be. There is nothing shameful about lusting over the one you're with. No woman will ever get me like you do."

"Why now, then? Why did you wait, and why did you treat me so coldly?"

Moving my hands to her hips, I glide them up her stomach, touching over the feminine roundness there. Fuck, she is every wet dream and spank bank come true. Each inch of her body looks like I sculpted it just for me.

"Because I didn't think you were ready. You're young and free, and I didn't want to hold you back."

"How would you hold me back? You didn't think I'd want you?"

Ivy doesn't even know her own seductiveness. With that simple question, it sounded like she was asking me to fuck her right there, take her like a mad man. "Baby, when you're mine, I don't take that lightly. I'll possess you. I'll own every inch of this body. You'll do what I say, and you'll be mine to do whatever I want. You'll become a part of me. Are you really ready for that?"

"Will you ever hurt me?" She tilts her head and bites her lip.

Wait... does she want that? "I would never hit you. Maybe a really good spanking with a hard fucking, but I would never hurt you. I just want you to belong to me solely. I don't want you to want anyone but me."

"I don't. I have only ever wanted you."

"No, I want you to desire me so much that it affects your day. You can't focus unless I'm in your presence. I want you at my feet, sucking my cock every damn night."

Her eyes go wide and her body jolts forward. "Yeah, like that," I praise her body for reacting to me.

"I can do that. I want that. The idea of being owned by you feels like the only right thing in my life. But..."

"But what?" I murmur, holding her eyes with mine.

"But is it reciprocated? Will I own you in return? Will I possess you, own every inch of your body? Will you do what I say and be mine to do whatever I want? Because I want you to be that for me too," she confesses.

"Baby, you already do. Since day one, you've owned me. Since the second you stepped into my office, you've possessed my body and soul. There hasn't been another woman since, and will never be one ever again after you," I tell her. Can't she see the truth written in my face? "You have to promise something to me before we start this."

She nods, leaning over on her own and kissing my neck then jaw. "Anything."

I groan, thrusting up into her, my cock wanting so badly to be inside her. "You can never leave me. I own you, Ivy."

She gulps, leaning back just enough to bring our faces within inches of each other. "If what you said is true and I own you too, then deal... Dr. Sage."

There is finality in her voice, and I know she's all in. "Look at you. You're topping me right now, Ivy."

She smiles wickedly, a look of confidence that is beautiful on her. Placing a soft kiss next to my ear, she whispers, "Help me get dressed?"

Her question catches me off guard and I laugh. "What? Why? We aren't done here. I still have to eat you for hours."

She blushes when she rocks back. "I would love that,

but Jenika and I have plans tonight. I promised her we would go to a club."

"No," I bite out, flipping us so I'm on top and my lips collide with hers in a brutal kiss.

She gives in for a moment, her body going completely lax beneath me as we share our first real kiss, but then she shakes her head. "Owen, I promised. I have to. We haven't had a girls' night in a while." Her hands timidly explore me with slight trepidation. They crawl up the back of my shirt, and she drags her nails ever so gently along the muscles of my lower back.

"You have to work tomorrow," I remind her, trying to think of anything that'll keep her here with me.

She giggles. "Yes, Daddy."

"Don't you sass me, Ivy." My voice promises punishment.

"You have to let me go. I promise to give you all my attention tomorrow. Maybe I might even come into your office between patients to steal some kisses."

I bite her neck then suck, marking my territory for all men to see she's taken. "Fine. But tomorrow, you come to the office early and I want to work on getting you comfortable. I want you on my desk before I get there, with no panties. You will send me a picture before I come in. Full cunt and all."

Her breath hitches. "I don't know if I can do that."

"Which part?"

"Both."

"For my eyes only. Remember it's you and me, and your body is not shameful. Say it," I tell her.

She shakes her head.

"Ivy, say it or I will not let you leave here without eating you out until you scream your forfeit."

"But Jenika—"

"I don't care. You know me better than that."

"Fine. I'll do it. But you can't let anyone see it."

"Another thing, baby." I let out a low rumble in my chest of annoyance. "I won't fucking share you."

Before she can protest, I lean in and kiss her, stealing the words right out of her mouth.

She's mine.

CHAPTER 11

Ivy

In twenty-four hours, my world flipped upside down.

Owen has declared his desire for me, claiming me during my appointment and then climbing in through my window, telling me the most raw, intimate, and nearly psychotic confessions. He told me things that made me question all my fears and phobias, challenged them and surprisingly had me heated in deep-rooted passion.

I want it so bad. I want everything he's offering me. I never thought I would agree to be owned, but with him... I want to be everything he wants and more. I want to be possessed.

"I look like an idiot. I shouldn't wear this."

"Take that back. Now, Ivy." He slaps my ass and I yelp, turning and peering up at him.

"Ouch." I rub at my bottom, and he pushes me up against the wall, caging me in with his arms on either side of my head.

"Take it back. I won't let you criticize yourself. Phobia or not. You look beautiful, and if I weren't trying to get you to see how perfect your body is, then I wouldn't let you out of this house."

"What? So I do look stupid?"

He leans, nipping at my lip. "You are way smarter than that, Ivy. I wouldn't let you leave, because no other man should see you like this. You look like a walking wet dream, and every man there tonight is going to want you."

"I don't want that. I only want you to see me." My hands reach up to stroke across his abs.

He hisses. "If you want to leave tonight, then stop tempting me. Show your body off with pride, just don't share it. Got it, Ivy?"

I nod, the heat between my legs, growing with his demand. "Yes, sir." I lick the spot on my lip he nipped. When he kisses me again, it turns passionate, our desire igniting all over again, but it's short-lived when my phone rings.

"Jenika," I whisper, and he lets me go, but his eyes stay on me like a predator's. "Hey. Sorry, I just need to put on some lipstick and grab my bag. We can't be out too late tonight. I have to work early."

"Ugh, did Dr. Sage call you in?"

"Yes, he did. I have to be there an hour and half early, so I can only have a few drinks."

"Fine! Hurry up and get here. I'm waiting and I got us a table. The perks of showing up before 9:00 p.m.!" she hollers over the loud music.

"Okay. I'll be there. See you soon." I hang up, turning toward Owen. "I have to go. She's waiting on me." I whisper, delicately grasping his shirt and pulling myself closer to him. "I don't want to, but I have to."

"I haven't been able to get you alone, and now when I do, you have to leave me. Fuck, you have me by the damn balls."

I blush, his growl arousing me. "I know. About the leaving part, I mean. Not the balls," I ramble. "But tomorrow, you can have me all to yourself. At work, we can flirt secretly. You can watch me like you want to and know I will be itching for you to take me." The last part comes out as a whimper, since he wastes no time lapping at my neck, biting the long column, and that causes a shiver to overcome my whole body.

"Tomorrow, you need to be early. I'm not messing around, Ivy. Don't make me wait," he demands, and I feel that threat deep inside me.

"Yes, sir. I promise."

With one last hard kiss to my lips, he fucks my mouth with his tongue and then pushes away. "Do not misbehave. Go now, Ivy." He grips my ass and pushes me toward my door. I go on shaky legs and enjoy the feeling of his eyes raking me over, taking me in as if I'm irresistible.

We don't say anything; instead, he leaves me with a slow burn, real anticipation burning through me for the coming twelve hours. It'll be pure torture, but I would be lying if I said I didn't crave it.

The music is so loud I can barely hear myself think, and that's all I want to do. My thoughts are clouded with all things Owen. I feel every inch of my skin that he touched tonight burning, and I can't soothe the sting. I want him, yet I'm terrified of what I will have to do to give in to our desire.

"That guy over there is staring at you with real fuck-me

eyes. Maybe you could fuck him sideways—pretend he's Dr. Sage. Get that practice in, baby girl," Jenika teases.

I roll my eyes and sip the margarita I've been nursing for nearly an hour. We danced until I was covered in a light sheen of sweat and laughing so hard my abs are sure to be bruised. I need it, the free feeling of being myself while reveling in the fact that everything I've always desired is becoming mine. "No, thank you. He's kind of creepy. Real serial killer vibes."

Throwing her head back, she lets out a throaty laugh and I can't help but smile along with her.

"Besides, I have to leave soon. It's been fun, but Dr. Sage needs me early tomorrow."

"Ugh, he's a buzz kill. If you two end up being together, please tell him not to suck the life out of you."

"I hope he sucks my fucking soul right out through my c-u-next-Tuesday." I cover my mouth, not believing I actually said that.

Jenika's eyes widen, and this time she topples over, holding her stomach in her fit of laughter. "Oh my God, Ivy! Did you just say that? Who are you and just how much tequila is in that damn margarita?"

No, really. Where did that come from? That is not something I would just say. How much alcohol is in this drink? Before I can answer either of those questions, the light next to my camera on my phone flashes on the table. I give her a goofy look and check my message.

HunterNumberNeighbor: Did I scare you away? I came thinking about you, and you ghosted me. Not too good for my ego. No, really. Where did you go, lovely Ivy?

Shit. I totally forgot. I'm really losing my footing right now.

Me: I couldn't do it. I'm sorry. I like you, Hunter, as a friend, but I'm in love with Owen. I couldn't do that with you. Please say you don't hate me. *watery-eyes emoji

HunterNumberNeighbor: What if he doesn't end up coming after you? Would you consider me then? What if you end up leaving him? How about then? *big smile emoji.

I visibly relax in my seat, so glad he isn't calling me every cock-tease name in the book.

Me: Even if Owen didn't want me, I wouldn't stop wanting him. I would be celibate and single before I ever thought of another man replacing him. Sorry, sweet number neighbor. Friends?

HunterNumberNeighbor: Ouch, friend-zoned. What a lucky man to have such a loyal woman. I'm jealous. But I get it.

Me: He's my everything. I plan to make him love me no matter what I do. He said he wanted me and I'm his, but that could be temporary or a ruse to get me in bed. But I won't stop until he wants me forever.

HunterNumberNeighbor: What would you do for him? Tell me everything you would be too afraid to tell him.

I look around, noticing that at some point while I was texting, Jenika had a gentlemen join her, talking her ear off and keeping her distracted. It makes me miss Owen. I want his body heat against me, touching me and filling me.

Me: Friends don't get to tell, so I guess my secrets are safe with you. I would do anything. Tie myself to his bed naked, even with my fear. I would lie there and beg him to want me. To keep me. I

would do anything emotionally and physically for him. He just has to ask.

HunterNumberNeighbor: Fuck. You are every man's dream woman. Men can say they don't want someone crazy and clingy, but we do. What I wouldn't give to have you crawling to me and begging for me to love you. How beautiful would that be?

I smirk, glad I'm only ever going to tell *him* this. I could never tell Owen. Sure, he has a dirty, dominant, possessive, and wild side, but there is no way he is this kind of crazy. I'm my own brand of psychotic, I guess. And though I will show him this side if I need to, I pray I never have to.

Me: You would run, I promise. Goodnight, number neighbor. Talk to you tomorrow.

All this talk makes me miss Owen, so I cut the conversation there and open a new message to the man I want to talk to most.

Me: I need you and can't stop thinking about what happened today. Are you sure you want me and weren't like... drunk or something today? LOL

My insecurities come out full on with all but a flashing neon sign, and I try to cover it with a joke like I always do.

Dr. Sage: Don't ever question my desire and need for you. I won't be easy with that cunt when I prove my point.

My core clenches and my whole body heats up again, a tingle starting in my toes and wrapping all the way up my spine.

Me: I don't want to go home alone tonight. If you want me, then you would be with me tonight. Calling your bluff hard, sir.

I hold my breath, wondering how he will take my sense of humor. I'm not used to speaking to him, much less outside of work, and even lesser in a lover's capacity. My humor is the one thing I've always genuinely liked about myself. I don't know what I'd do if he disliked that part of my personality.

Thankfully, I don't have to ponder that thought for very long.

Dr. Sage: Call it a night and get that beautiful ass home now.

I grin at his assertiveness. Guess he likes that side of me after all. And Dr. Owen Sage calling me beautiful does tremendous things for my ego, and sets off a flutter... in my vagina.

Me: I'm so hot for you right now.

I get up from the table, and when Jenika's eyes find mine and she sees the happy and anxious look on my face, her lips spread into a wicked smile.

"Getcha some, girl!" she calls out over the music as I start toward the exit, and my phone buzzes in my hand.

Dr. Sage: Ivy, control will be practiced tonight. You aren't ready for my cock in your virgin pussy. You'll get all of me except that tonight. Now get home. I'll meet you there.

My pussy clenches at his dirty words.

CHAPTER 12

Ivy

When I arrive home, he's on my front porch, his shoulder leaned next to the door, his ankles crossed, just like his arms. His crystal blue eyes are a laser as they stare into mine as I come up the steps, the plastic bag hanging from my forearm, and then he turns his wrist slightly toward himself, keeping his arms crossed while he glances down at his shiny watch.

"That took entirely too long," he states, his face annoyed but his eyes twinkling with mischief. I love this look on him, so used to seeing him scowl at work.

"I um... had to make a quick stop. Sorry for making you wait," I tell him, using my key to unlock the door and push it open, aware of him following me inside. It's almost a static feeling, the little hairs on my skin standing up and reaching toward his closeness.

He shuts the door, the deadbolt making an ominously loud clack as he turns it in place, making me jump. "I'm certain I told you to get home immediately," he murmurs, taking steps until his front is pressed to my back and he towers above me. If I leaned my head back, it'd rest on his wide, muscular chest.

I close my eyes so all my other senses can focus on the man behind me, and instantly I can smell his intoxicating cologne. The scent goes straight to my pussy, and I grow wet beneath my dress. I realize I still need to respond. "Trust me, it was for the best."

Before I know what's happening, he's already slid my plastic bag off my arm, holding it out of my reach when my eyes snap open and I swipe for it. As I turn to face him, he lifts a brow at me and smirks when I put my fists on my hips and tap my foot.

"Let's see what was so important that you had to disobey me, pretty girl," he says, and his voice is a mix of reprimand and curiosity, his tone light.

I pop my hip sassily, my lips twisting as I glare. I give in, knowing I won't be able to stop him, but I don't have to be happy about it. All I can do now is try my best to fight the heat climbing from my chest up into my cheeks.

Pulling the first item out of the bag, he holds it up so the lamp by my couch I left on so I wouldn't have to come home to a dark house lights it up. "Refreshing wipes," he reads, turning the package over and scanning the back. When his eyes meet mine, they don't look happy, but he doesn't say anything. Instead, he looks around for a moment, spotting the small wastebasket I have under the table with the lamp and tossing the feminine product in.

I bite my lip, staying silent as he pulls out the next item from the bag.

"Mouthwash," he says, his mouth twitching as if he's fighting a smile. This time, he places the travel-size bottle down on the kitchen island next to us instead of throwing it away, and then proceeds to do the same with each of the other products he pulls out. "Deodorant... a travel toothbrush... toothpaste... a half a bottle of water... aaand... I'm not sure what this is." He narrows his eyes, reading the little tube. "Oh, concealer." He then balls up the plastic bag and puts it into the wastebasket. When his eyes come to me again, he lifts a sexy brow. "Explain."

I huff, shoving my hair out of my face. "Really, Owen? It's not obvious?"

"Oh, it is. But I want to know what was going on in that pretty head of yours that made you think you needed to stop and stock up on toiletries when I was very clear in what I wanted you to do. Which was—Get. Home. Now."

My shoulders deflate like I've been scolded for doing something my parent specifically told me not to do, and the emotion is topped only by another much stronger one—embarrassment over having to say it out loud.

"Our texts." I huff again. "Our texts made me.... Well, your words were super-arousing, and they made me..."

"They made you what, Ivy?" He steps closer, mere inches away.

"They... they made me... wet. Like, soaked. To the point I could... smell myself." I whisper the last two words, my face flaming with mortification. I don't think I'll ever be able to look him in the eye again.

Until...

"Fuck," he growls, and he reaches between us to adjust his tented slacks.

My startled eyes find his heated ones.

"And the rest of it?" he prompts.

His reaction to my confession suddenly perks up my

confidence, not feeling so much like a reprimanded child anymore.

"I had a drink at the bar that left a bad taste in my mouth, and I thought if I thought my mouth tasted bad, then you probably would too. So I brushed my teeth and used the mouthwash in my car using the bottled water." Then I murmur, "Definitely need to remember to throw that McDonald's cup out tomorrow, since it's currently full of my spit."

And then he does something that curls my toes it's so delicious to witness. A smile takes over his entire handsome face and he throws his head back and laughs, a deep, hearty sound that comes from the depths of his belly. It takes my breath away, and my eyes even tear up a little at how beautiful he is when he laughs.

When he sobers, he asks, "And the concealer?"

"Oh, that was just because I'm almost out, so I figured since I was at Walgreens, I might as well grab it while I was there." I shrug.

The next thing I know, Owen lifts me up as if I weigh nothing and tosses me onto his shoulder, slapping my ass once and making me yelp as I try to catch my breath at the sudden change in altitude. "What are you doing?" I squeak.

"That was for not following orders," he says, and he begins moving in the direction of my bedroom.

I think.

I could be wrong though. Because my eyes have a front-row view of his impeccable ass, and I nearly drool watching the muscles work as he carries me... somewhere.

I actually pout when he takes hold of me in a way to swing me down off his shoulder, and I land on my soft mattress with a little bounce.

"First and foremost, Ivy. Do. Not. *Ever*. Try to hide your arousal from me. There is nothing on this earth I desire more than the juices from that tight little cunt," he rumbles, and his vulgar words make me gasp, my hand going to my throat daintily, as if I were wearing pearls.

"Owen," I breathe, shaking my head.

"Don't try to argue with me," he says, taking hold of the backs of my knees and spreading my legs with a jerk. The force of the movement pulls my ass to the edge of the bed, and I whimper at the dark look in his eyes as his knees lower to the floor. Without any warning, he reaches beneath my skirt and yanks my panties down and off, and to my mortification, he balls them in his fist and lifts it to his nose. He takes a deep inhale through his nose, and I wish the bed would just open up and swallow me whole as if I'm Johnny Depp in *Nightmare on Elm Street*.

His angry growl chills the marrow in my bones.

"What did you do? There's no way using those—" His face twists in disgust. "—wipes would have gotten rid of your scent so thoroughly."

I swallow. "I um... I.... The thought of going commando almost gave me a panic attack, thanks to my uh... you know, my gymnophobia. So I went to the drug store's bathroom, washed them with the hand soap, and dried them with the hand dryer. After cleaning myself up with the feminine wipes, I put them back on," I confess, watching him shake his head through my explanation.

"Second on our list of lessons—stay away from those wipes. The ones you picked out, while they may smell nice and perfumed, are not PH-balanced. They could fuck up this perfect, untouched pussy of yours and give you an infection. And never put anti-bacterial soap anywhere near this cunt again. It kills not only the bad bacteria, but the good kind too. The kind that keeps this delicious little slit a nice and healthy meal for me to eat," he tells me, and strokes his finger through my slick lower lips.

My breath comes out on a whoosh, and I feel so out of my element right now that I say the first thing that pops into my head. "It's almost like you're an expert on the subject. Are you a gynecologist or something?" I bite my lip to keep from letting out a nervous giggle.

"I'm an expert on all things you, Ivy. Fuck. My sweet, innocent Ivy." There's heat in his eyes, and it burns through me, igniting my body.

I don't have to be an expert on sex and lust to know the look of raw, ravenous want. "Do you want me, Owen?" I try to tempt him in a way I never have before, taking control of his desire for me. I bite my lip, a poor attempt at looking sexy, I'm sure, but it's something I've seen in every romance movie and read in every romance novel.

"I do. But you don't get to have my cock just yet. No, you're not ready to be made into my own personal sex addict."

I gulp, my cheeks flaring with heat. "I could never do that. Sex with you will be amazing, sure, but with my phobia, I don't think I'll ever be confident enough to let loose in that way." My words trail off and I drop my eyes to the floor.

"You have no idea. I will obliterate all your fears. In fact, you will be so hungry for my cock you won't be able to focus at work or have a conversation with anyone else without craving it. You won't be able to stand going without it multiple times a day. Don't doubt it, because when you doubt me, it only makes me more unstoppable. I will fuck you into submission, and you will eat those words like you'll eat my cock, Ivy. Nightly."

"Owen." My core clenches, his words offending me in all the right ways.

"On the bed, hike that dress, legs spread," he orders, and my heart plummets.

I shake my head, suddenly acutely aware of what's happening. My senses are on high alert, and I really can't bring my pulse back down to a healthy rate. "I can't. You scare me," I whisper.

"I should. That fear will turn into desire, but you have to trust that I know what you want. That you are safe with me."

There is something about the softness that overtakes his every feature. It eases his sharp edges, and it makes me feel like I'm right where I want to be. "Will you stop if I get too afraid?" I question, mustering every ounce of my courage to grab a fistful of his shirt. I pull him in so I can kiss the chiseled line of his jaw.

"You're all mine, Ivy, but in this life and in the bedroom, you own all of me. I'm at your mercy. You say when and you say how unless you want me to take control."

The complete trust and ownership he lays at my feet is enough to annihilate all doubt. "You own me, any way you want, in life and in the bedroom." I repeat his words back to him and solidify our promise.

"Good. Now do as I asked, baby." He rarely calls me pet names like that, so when he does, it turns me into straight mush.

"Yes, sir." Climbing on the bed, I do exactly as my doctor told me to.

CHAPTER 13

Ivy

"Owen!" I scream when he slaps my inner thigh for trying to close my legs when he gets close to me. I assume the position, and he moves in on me so very slowly, like a lion stalking its prey.

"Don't hide your body, Ivy. That is a feat we've already conquered, and I will not allow you to backslide. You're beautiful, a work of art, and nothing—not a single inch of you—should be hidden."

"Tell me that then, Owen. I need reassurance. I need words," I confess.

"Dirty talk, or just my words?" He circles my clit with a heavy hand, the pressure so raw and good I can't help but moan loudly.

My whole body shivers. "Both. Oh! So good!"

Then he slaps my clit hard, making me squeal in surprise. A wave of hot arousal floods my core, something

I wasn't expecting, and I fly up, my hands barely holding me up as I scream his name. "Owen! Oh my—fuck!"

He moves fast, dropping his mouth to my slit and eating it with an intensity so palpable that I roll into a fast-hitting orgasm. He's doing it. He's numbing my mind to anything other than the pleasure he can bring me.

"Fuck. There it is," he growls, making me quiver.

I look down at him as he laps at me, licking, sucking, and fucking his tongue into me. It's a sight that has my stomach tightening with a sensation I can't express. Owen is a part of me now, and I know I can't ever share what I am with anyone but him. I don't want to. I can't. I refuse it. We are one now.

"Wha—what? There's what?" I have a handful of his hair, but I massage his scalp gently.

"That natural scent, your creamy, luscious, wet cunt smell you tried to wash away. My favorite fucking scent that I own, Ivy." He growls again, biting my clit, and I come again. And somehow I know that most of it came from his crude but extremely sexy words.

He soothes me for a few minutes as my orgasm lasts longer this time, lapping at me softly, his eyes boring into mine, possessing me. My heavy-lidded eyes can't seem to leave his, and I know this is part of him trying to fix me. Part of him trying to get me to look intimacy right in the eye and own it. To claim my own sexuality and share it with him.

"I'm going to let you suck my cock, and then you're going to let me put you to bed."

I nod, my eyes still slightly open and my core still clenching and pulsing. I roll to my stomach and lift myself onto my knees—well, attempt to. And the euphoria running through my veins spikes my confidence enough to joke, "You've turned me to mush. Dickmatized me." I chuckle, and he slaps my ass before I turn to face him.

"You're funny. Sated and still sassy." He smiles.

"I like to believe I'm quite the lady." I purse my lips, and he bites his bottom one.

"You turn me on... so badly, so ferociously, Ivy. Now, be a good girl and undo my pants and pull out my cock. I won't tell you what to do after that. You will learn and do what you want. I want to see you trust your sexuality."

"You're giving me the control now?" I'm both nervous at the responsibility and excited.

"Yes." And like he promised he would, he says nothing else. Instead, he takes my hair and puts it behind my shoulders, barely grazing my skin but making my body shiver. Undoing his button first then his zipper, I gulp once and look up at him, hoping he will tell me what he wants, but he just gives me a dark, sexy grin.

Please, let me do it right again, like I did in the exam room, I pray. My adrenaline was rushing so strongly then I don't really remember what I'd done that made him come so easily.

I pull his boxer briefs down and free his large, thick, veiny cock from its confines and choke on a breath. The first time stole my breath, but this second time stops my heart. I can only imagine what will happen any other time I see it.

"Owen, I want to please you. I want to give you everything. You make me feel this need to share myself with you in a way that only you will ever get to see." I lay out all my thoughts and feelings... and he says nothing, making that raw feeling so much more palpable and intense. All I can do is continue in order to fill the heavy silence. "I want you to own not just my body, but everything else. I don't want anyone seeing me the way you do. I want you to own my laughs." I lift his shirt and kiss the deep left groove of his V. "I want you to own my secrets." I kiss the right. "I want you to own the things that make me happiest."

I peer up, and he just watches me, his eyes casted down and his chin lifted in a most stoic and powerful way. It melts me. Destroys me.

"I don't want anyone to ever see me, touch me, or feel me the way you do," I whisper with finality.

He grips my hair then takes control, no words as he brings my mouth to his cock and pushes in brutally—but so fucking beautifully. "I will own all of those things and so much more. Suck my cock and show me those words actually mean something."

And then to my complete embarrassment, I start to cry, but his touch is so intense and filled with ownership I have wanted for so long I just can't help it. The tears fall, and he knows they aren't sad ones or from the brute force in which he is making me suck his cock, but because I've completely surrendered myself to my love.

"You look beautiful when you cry and suck my cock. Oh, fuck! Slow down, Ivy. I need you to take your time. Your hot little mouth is going to make me come." He tilts my head and pushes deeper, his crown hitting the back of my mouth. My throat opens as best as it can to accommodate him. "I thought those pouty fuck-me lips couldn't look more beautiful, but one day you'll see the way they look wrapped around my cock. One day, I'll get you over your fears and I'll record you sucking me off, me fucking every beautiful orifice of your body. You're going to learn how to fuck yourself on my cock and not just give *me* pleasure whenever I want it, but whenever you want it too, beautiful. Fuck. I'm going to come. Swallow it all, Ivy."

My desire to please him increases tenfold and I suction around him, giving him long, slow pulls. I flatten my tongue and let it rub rhythmically along the underside of his shaft, and he lets out a primitive growl, a moan that an alpha would make when they're mating, staking their claim. And in this moment, I just want to have him inside me—taking my virginity and possessing me completely.

"Ivy, damn it. I love you. You belong to me. Open your throat and take every drop."

My hair stands on end. He just said he loves me. Owen loves me. The man I love loves me back. And with a few more unsteady thrusts of his hips, he comes, his salty taste gliding down my throat. I moan, painfully aroused by the knowledge that I'm bringing him this much pleasure.

When his tremors stop and I'm sure he's done, I slowly pull back, peering up at him. I use one finger and wipe the corner of my now swollen lips. "I—I love you too, Owen."

He grips my neck and tilts my head up, and there is something in his eyes I can't quite explain. There seems to be a glimmer of sadness there, and I want to say something about it, but in this moment, perfect silence is what feels right. I will get it out of him tomorrow. I will dig deeper, but for now, I enjoy the feel of him tightening his grip on my neck as he softly pulls my ass from my calves to meet my lips to his in a demanding kiss. We do this for hours, long hours that pass too quickly until I fall asleep and wake to his absence.

CHAPTER 14

Owen

Today.

I have to tell Ivy today that I'm Hunter.

I can't wait any longer. I refuse to take her, to sink myself deep inside her virgin heat, until she knows the truth, until there is nothing on my conscience. So I must tell her today I'm her number neighbor.

Never in my life have I felt guilty, especially when it came to a woman. Of course, I've never wanted to spend more than one night with a female before. It was the watching, the chase I always enjoyed. And once I figured her out and got what I wanted, the appeal dissolved. I had no use for her any longer, so it was on to the next.

But not Ivy. Never Ivy. The more and more I discover about her, the more I want to keep her. Always. I know in my heart my desire for her will never disappear. I'll never get enough of her. She is the very reason I breathe. Without her, I'd have no reason to exist. We are meant to live this life together, and I refuse to get any further into our relationship without it being free and clear of all deception. From the moment I tell her the truth and then on, there will never be anything but honesty between us.

Me: Any update on the good doctor?

I know, I know. I shouldn't be using Hunter as a way of digging into Ivy's feelings about me, but I'm addicted to how open she is when she thinks she's speaking to someone she'll never meet. I can only hope she's this way with me once we become more familiar with each other.

There's a soft knock on my office door and then it opens just as my text notification goes off, and I see my beauty walk in. The tone is still ringing out as she closes it behind her, her eyes landing on my cell as I quiet it and put it in the top drawer of my desk.

"I came to see if you'd maybe... like to have lunch together today. I know you bring yours every day, so I made sure to pack mine too, so we could um... eat together," she gets out, and I smile.

"I'd love that," I reply, spinning around in my rolling chair to grab my lunch from the mini fridge behind my desk. I pull the meal prep out of its bag, take the lid off, and place it in the small microwave on top of the fridge. Setting it to heat for one minute, I push start. But nothing happens.

I glance over my shoulder as Ivy takes a seat on the other side of my desk, feeling her closeness like a physical thing, before trying to start the microwave again. I push the button over and over, but nothing happens.

Her quiet voice comes. "Maybe it's like a cell phone. Just turn it off and then back on again."

I chuckle, but stand and unplug it from the wall before

plugging it back in and trying to start it once more. But it still doesn't work.

Ivy stands from her seat, reaching out her hand. "I can go heat it up for you in the break room if you'd like?"

My first instinct is to tell her no, that I'd just eat it cold so I wouldn't have to be without her for even a moment. But seeing the sweet look on her face, the one that shows me exactly what her words said in her text about wanting to be helpful and please me, I give in.

"Thank you. That would really help me out," I tell her, and the smile that spreads across her face could light up this entire block. She takes the container and leaves my office.

Knowing I have at least a minute before she comes back, I read the text she sent before coming in. She must've sent it right outside my door for the notification to go off as she entered.

Ivy: I'm going to see if he'll have lunch with me. Wish me luck!

Me: You've got this!

I smile to myself, reading back through our past messages, when another one comes in just as I shut it off again, the text tone ringing out.

Ivy: He said yes! And even let me heat his lunch up for him when his microwave wouldn't work.

I go to respond, but hear something from the front of my office. I look up to see Ivy standing in the open doorway, and it's then I realize she'd left it open on her way out to the break room.

Her eyes narrow as she tilts her head to the side, my meal in one hand and her cell in the other. I watch, my heart pounding in my chest as her thumb slides across her screen, unlocking her phone. She hits one button… then another, and my eyes close in defeat as my phone rings in my grip.

But that must not be enough for her. When I open my eyes again, her face is full of disbelief. She moves her thumb along the touchscreen once more then pulls it up to her ear, calling Hunter's number for the very first time.

And when my cell starts blaring, all I can do is answer it, holding it up to my ear and murmuring, "Let me explain."

CHAPTER 15

Owen

She's gone.

She dropped my food to the floor, the sound echoing much like the hollow sound my heart makes when she leaves me.

It takes me a minute to sprint into action. Finally, I open my drawer, grab my wallet and keys, and take off after her. That's all I can do, and I curse myself for not fucking telling her when I had the damn chance.

"Cancel my afternoon! I'm not feeling well," I bite out at Jenika, not stopping when she asks me to wait. I have one mission, and that is to get to my Ivy.

Fuck. I felt nothing but defeat over my utter betrayal toward her when she looked up at me, broken and abused by my manipulation. And I deserve all the wrath she's bound to release on me. She is peeling out of the parking lot as I slide into my Audi, already running thanks to the push of a button on my fob, and I take off after her. I take note of the dark clouds that have formed in the sky above, and I pray they don't open up and storm down on us while she's driving so upset.

I hit her name on my dash as I weave in and out of cars, keeping my eye on hers just a few vehicles ahead of me. "Pick up, Ivy. Fuck, pick up!" I curse when she takes a sharp turn and the car in front of me slams on his brakes, leaving me even farther behind. I maneuver quickly, swerving out from behind the stopped car and speeding in front of him, cutting him off, and paying no mind to his loud horn.

I call and call. Over and over again from my phone—well, Hunter's phone—and get nothing. I do it the whole way until I'm pulling up in front of her place. She is getting out of her car, and I barely throw mine in Park before climbing out, almost reaching her. But she was too far ahead of me and is able to slam the door shut and lock it just as I hurl both fists into it and growl, "Ivy! Fuck, baby. Come on and let me explain. I know you will understand. Don't push me out."

In this moment, I realize just how much she owns me. I'm weakening like putty in her hands and then pooling at her feet. Something so out of character for a man of my stature and pride. I don't chase or grow weak for women. It's the other way around. But for my sweet Ivy, it's all the complete opposite.

"Ivy. Let me in."

"No! You betrayed me. I... I trusted you," she sobs from the other side of the wood.

A sharp pain sears through me and my voice lowers. "I know. I fucked up. I let you down, but you don't understand the man I am and what you fucking do to me, lovely. I'm fucking crazy about you. Ivy, I would do anything for you. I would fucking kill for you." The last part comes out in a dangerous growl, an edge to my voice.

"Owen... please. I can't." Her resolve is shattering, and I see the small window I have to explain it all and trap her in my hands. "Go to your bedroom window, baby. I promise to make you forgive me."

She doesn't say anything, and I place my ear to the door to listen. A long, pregnant pause goes by before I hear her floorboards creaking under her feet as she moves to the bedroom. I move fast, the rain that threatened to fall now coming down in pouring waves and soaking me within seconds. I round her house and come to the side where her bedroom window is.

She stands in the center of the room, her arms wrapped tightly around her waist, protecting herself. That hurts. I caused her that fear and vulnerability she's feeling, when I should be the one in there holding her together and bringing her back to solid ground.

I take a minute to catch my breath, and once it evens out, I take slow steps toward her window, and her red, teary eyes watch me like I watch her. "I'm not a sane person when it comes to you, Ivy. You make me fucking crazy. You've turned me into the type of man a woman should fear."

I see her throat move, a hard swallow as she visibly trembles. A fresh wave of tears begins to fall, but I know what they are. They aren't tears of heartbreak. They're tears of understanding and fear. Ivy knows what I mean, because like she told me when she thought I was Hunter, she would do anything to catch and keep me.

"I've stalked you, lovely Ivy. Every fucking night for months, I have sat outside your window and watched you, craved you, desired you." I'm now at the glass pane, my large hand rising to press my palm against it as the rain drenches me, rivulets falling from my hair down my face. "I knew what my desire for you could do, and I had to make sure you were ready. I had to get into that beautiful fucking head, Ivy. I had to. I love you, and if you try to push me out, you will regret it. I won't stop. I will follow you anywhere you go and make sure you always remember you are mine. Do you get that? Do you see why I had to do it this way?"

She tightens her grip and nods. I see her lips move, and it reads a whimpered *yes*.

"I bought the house next to you. I watched you and learned who you were. I fell in love with you and you became mine. Unlock this window and let me apologize to you. Let me show you what my love and obsession can be like. Please open the window, baby."

She waits, the last thread of resistance hanging there. After what is only a few moments but feels like hours, she takes slow, hesitant steps. Right when she reaches the window, she raises her hand to unlock it... but stops and stands back.

No. Please! That ounce of hope I had moments ago is fleeting. I can't lose her.

"Ivy."

"No. You watched me, because you wanted me. Now I want you to feel the pain of what I felt when I found out you lied." Her voice is just loud enough for me to hear as it elevates.

"What? Ivy, you need to open the window now. I'm not opposed to breaking it—" I stop when she pulls her chiffon shirt off in one swoop, leaving her in a lace white bra. I choke and swallow past the dryness in my speechless throat.

"You want me, don't you? So badly you would ruin it with your lies?" She unbuckles and unzips her dress slacks, letting them slide effortlessly off her curvy hips, those panties matching her bra, making my cock so damn hard.

"Ivy," I warn.

"You deserve the payback, to watch me bare what you've proclaimed is yours. See me come without you."

Fuck. She reaches behind her and unhooks her bra, letting it fall to the floor so her beautiful, lush tits can assault my eyes. They display her arousal, her nipples hard, the skin of her chest flushed with lust. She is turned on, her gymnophobia nowhere in sight. Did her discovery turn her on and silence her fears?

"I will lie on this bed and come to the thought of *Hunter*. It'll make you so angry knowing I'm fucking myself to the idea of a man I didn't know was you."

I punch the hard siding of her house, just next to the window. "Ivy. Don't you dare touch that cunt without me, and don't you *ever* think of anyone but me," I hiss. My anger is rising, my jealousy boiling irrationally. There are black dots dancing in my vision, yet my cock is so painfully hard that it just may rip through my slacks.

"He knew me best, after all." And with that, she turns and walks to the bed and lies down, her lace-covered cunt on full display for me as she props her feet on the bed.

I watch my worst nightmare and greatest desire unfold in front of me. Framing her dainty fingers along her clit on the outside of her panties, she starts to rub herself in circles, her other hand gripping her breast.

"Ivy!" I growl while slamming my fist against her window frame.

She increases the speed, knowing exactly what she's doing to me. Suddenly, I'm faced with blinding rage and a mission I can't stop. Putting my hands on the lip of her window, I pull up with all my strength. Within seconds, the lock on the window snaps and splinters onto the floor. I lift the window and climb in. This has her halting her beautiful assault on her cunt and trying to scurry off the other side of her bed, but I stalk to her briskly and grab her ankles.

Yanking and flipping her over, I pull her to the edge of the bed. "Owen! Oh my God!"

"How dare you, you naughty girl." I slap her ass so hard the sound cracks in the air, overpowering the heavy rain falling outside the window and making her squeal.

"How dare *you*! You stalked me. You lied to me. You abused your power!" she spits out, sitting up then trying to get away, but I don't let her. I push her down on the bed and put her hands above her head, her wrists locked in my tight grip.

"Admit it. You love that I was so crazy over you that I infiltrated every part of your life. I got inside you every way I could and watched you in a way that made you most vulnerable and most mine. You can use your anger as a cover up for your desire, but make no mistake—I own you and can do whatever I want with you. I will never stop watching you and possessing you, Ivy." I grip her chin when she moans, her back arching and her beautiful breasts pushing against my chest.

"No, I hate that. I hate that I love how psycho and maniacal you are. I love you, Owen, and you hurt me in all the ways I hate to admit that I want."

"I know I did, lovely Ivy, but I did it because I knew it was what we both wanted. Let me make it up to you. Show you I'm sorry with my cock," I whisper in her ear, and she shivers.

She whimpers, "Tell me what you did while you watched me."

"You were fucking made for me. Stand up," I demand first, helping her with her hand in mine. She stands in front of me, ready to hear what I did before I finally claim her, her curvy, breathtaking body on display for me. "I watched you, came to you. My cock ached every night as I stroked it while stalking you. I fucked my hand every night for this body. You brought me to my knees." I turn her around. "Bend over."

I push her between her shoulder blades, and she bends over the bed, her arms supporting her. "I saw you bend over every night, just like this, your cunt glistening for me. You left your curtains open, because you wanted me to see you. You must have felt my desire for you, wanted me to lust after you... and I did. This beautiful pussy." I reach between her legs and thrum her clit.

She jolts forward and cries, "Owen!"

"You didn't know I was the one watching though, Ivy, and that makes me both aroused and angry, because other men could have seen your body in a way only I should." I spank her ass and she screams out. "Tell me you're sorry for being such a naughty girl."

"I—I... oh! I'm sorry, Owen."

I use my oxford-covered foot to gently kick her ankles apart, and when I have a better advantage, I slap her clit.

"Ah!" she squeals, her thighs trembling.

"Tell me you forgive me, lovely. Fuck, this cunt is so damn wet for this." I circle her clit with even pressure, just enough to keep her on the edge but not enough to make her come.

"I forgive you. Please, Owen," she pleads breathlessly.

"What do you want, beautiful?" I pull her up, her back

to my front, and I reach around to grab her full, luscious tits, pulling at the hardened tips.

"I want you to take me. Please. I'm not above begging."

"Then beg," I growl, pinching her nipples.

She jolts forward. "Please! Owen. I can't wait anymore. Please!" she lets out in a rush, her hands finding mine on her flesh and kneading her heavy tits with me.

"Lie on the bed and don't say a word. Legs spread, knees up."

CHAPTER 16

Owen

She nods, and I release her. On shaky legs, she turns and assumes the position. I undress, first removing my tie ever so slowly, making her wait. She watches, her eyes hooded as I unbutton my tight-fitted dress shirt next. When I remove it, she lets out a whimper. I give her a cocky smirk. I know how hard I work to keep my body fit and defined, and seeing her appreciate and lust over it is the greatest payoff. Next, I toe off my shoes and remove my pants and socks. Once I'm standing completely bare in front of her, I let her gaze rake over my body, enjoying each hard inch of me.

She takes that lip between her teeth, and my cock grows that one last final inch, fully erect and ready for her. I don't think I've ever been this hard for any woman. I may be the master in this relationship, but she owns and controls my body just as much. "You won't be needing condoms. I will never use those with you. Got it?"

She nods, her wide eyes looking at me with overwhelming desire. "Yes, sir. I could get pregnant though. I never went and picked up the prescription you gave me for birth control." She blushes bashfully.

I give a throaty, almost evil-sounding laugh. "Oh, Ivy, that's not a concern I have. Your cunt and your body are mine to take, and if my come gets you pregnant, then you'll never be able to leave. I wasn't lying when I said I would own you completely."

"Oh my God." She gives a sweet laugh. "How do you say such crazy... literally *insane* things, yet it just makes me want you even more?" She shakes her head. "And who knew that number neighbor game would get me pregnant?" she teases, trying to mask her nerves.

"Do you want me to shut that sassy mouth with my cock again, lovely?"

She giggles, the sound so damn beautiful. I listened to it from afar for so long at work, and now it's all mine.

"After you make me come with your cock deep inside me," she whispers, her confidence evidently growing with her arousal, and my brow rises.

"Good girl. I see you're starting to come out from under your fear." I climb between her legs, hovering above her and lining my cock up with her entrance.

"You make me feel brave," she breathes as she looks between us at where the head of my dick nudges her wetness.

"Good. Because the things I will teach you over time will really make you feel brave. Now, deep breath and let me lead. Relax your body." We lock eyes, and all this time of wanting her comes rushing in as I enter just an inch. Instantly, her eyes water, and that weakens me. I would usually be vile with my dirty talk, but I want to make her first time special. "I love you, Ivy."

Her tears slide down the side of her temple and into her chestnut hair. I kiss each corner of her eyes, her nose, and then her beautiful lips, giving her another inch. "I—ouch. I love you too."

"This is going to hurt, baby, but relax as much as you can and let me in. I promise I will make this good for you."

With that, she forces herself to go limp, her core opening up for me, but she's still unbelievably tight. I'm about to breach her virginity and I join our lips again, giving her long, breathy kisses, our tongues intimately massaging one another. Her taste mixes with mine. My hell, she's destroying me.

"Lovely Ivy, I'm going to go all the way. Tell me you're ready."

She nods. "Yes, Owen. Please."

With that, I reach down and wrap my hand around her dainty knee to pull it up as high as it can go beside her, opening her up more, and then I thrust hard.

"Oh! Oh my God!" she screams, and I halt all movement below, my mouth finding her neck, her chin, her lips, and anywhere else I can reach.

"You are so tight. You can't fit all of me. Goddamn, you should see how your cunt is trying to take each inch." I look between us, the image violent, my huge cock inside her, her lips gripping my girth. It's an image I will never forget. "Shit, you're so fucking perfect. You ready for me to move?"

She releases her lip that her teeth captured, and when she does, I see the faintest hint of red. She bit it so hard she drew blood. I lean down and lick it up with a swipe of my tongue, and her eyes widen.

"Owen! You're a madma—"

My dick jumps inside her at the coppery taste and the look in her eyes, cutting her off. Keeping one hand beside her head to balance while hovering above her as my other hand grips her hip, I groan as she moves, riding my cock while beneath me. Her hands grip my biceps, her back arched and her head thrown back as I glide in and out, her pain dissipating to pure euphoria. "I'm going to come inside this tight cunt if you keep moaning like that and gripping me so tight. You're insatiable and deadly. Do you have any idea what I'm willing to do to you and for you, Ivy?"

"I know. You make me just as mad. I can't believe you're mine. I love you, Owen. Oh! Just like that. I think you're... you're going to make me come."

"You're a natural. You only need my cock to make you come. You are a rare gift and you're all mine." Most women can't come from just vaginal penetration. But my lovely Ivy can, and in that moment, I vow to keep this cunt coming every night. "Oh fuck! Take my cum and come for me, now!"

She screams my name, her nails digging into my back, definitely drawing blood, and I swear my entire body convulses. I love how visceral this is. She can take the sweet and the brutal. Ivy was made for me. Designed by the gods just for me. I couldn't have made her more perfect if I hand-selected each and every aspect of who she is.

"Lovely Ivy, you are finally mine."

When her breathing comes to a normal rate and her tremors finally subside, her hands cup my face. "Thank goodness for stalkers and number neighbors," she says with a smile and a satisfied sigh, and I give her hip a possessive squeeze.

CHAPTER 17

Owen

As I fall to the side, pulling her with me to tuck her tightly to my side, I revel in the feel of her burrowing even closer. Our bodies slick with sweat, I reach down and pull the sheet over us so she doesn't get chilled as the AC kicks on.

I feel tension in the air, and I glance down to see her face full of questions, but I have no fear that she doubts anything between us, because her body is still melted against mine. So I ask, "What is it, my love?"

She reaches up to play with the light hair on my chest, glancing into my eyes before watching her fingers instead. "Will you tell me everything? Like... when did it all start? Your... stalking, I mean. And was... was it only me?"

"I will never be anything but honest with you from here on out. That's my promise to you," I say as a prelude.

She winces. "That can't be good," she murmurs.

"I've stalked before. Other women have caught my *very brief* attention, but once I watched them, learned a few things about them, I grew bored. You're the only one I've ever stalked for more than a week," I tell her.

Her lips twist pensively. "Did you have sex with them?"

"A few, yes. But they were strangers. One-night stands. They never even knew my real name."

"Were you Hunter to them too?" she asks, jealousy lacing her tone.

I use my index finger to lift her chin and look her in the eyes. "Never. I was only ever Hunter to you. After all, it's my real name. Something about giving you a fake name, even when I was being dishonest by not telling you it was me, rubbed me the wrong way. I always wanted you to know it was me you were talking to."

"Hunter is your real name?" Her brow furrows.

"Owen Hunter Sage."

She smiles, her eyes finally relaxing. "Tell me the rest?"

I turn her head so her cheek lays on my chest as I begin stroking her hair, feeling her puff of breath as she purrs. "I wanted you the moment you stepped foot into my office during your interview. You were smart, said all the right things, and God, so beautiful, so innocent. I knew I had to have you. But little did I know, as I followed you home the first time, how completely obsessed I would become. It wasn't just watching to sate my curiosity. I wanted to know every last detail of your entire existence. But there was only so much I could learn just by watching through your window. Even after buying the house next door so I could be as close to you as possible without you knowing, I could only come to my own conclusions about who you were inside by observing from the outside. So when I saw your post—and yes, I read all your public posts on social media, which gave me brief glimpses of who you are—about the number neighbor game, I knew that was my in. So I found out who owned that phone number and bought it from them. And well... now here we are."

She stays silent for so long, so relaxed against me, that I think she might've fallen asleep. But then I hear that sweet giggle.

"What?" I prompt.

"I can't believe all the things I said... the things I did... thinking I'd never meet Hunter in real life. Things at the time I thought I'd be mortified if you knew about. And now, I can't help but be grateful it was you all along. There's not some stranger out there who knows my dirty little secrets. And at the same time, I don't have to go through trying to hide those things from you now, because you already know," she says, tilting her head up to look at me, relief in her eyes.

"I want you to always be with me the way you were in our messages. Talk to me about anything. Tell me your every fear, and I swear on my life I'll do everything I can to banish them. Confess your every desire, and I promise to fulfill each one. I'm yours, and you're mine." I trace along her delicate jawline then across her plump bottom lip.

She smiles at me. "We'll need to think of more shades of green," she says oddly, and I lift a brow in question. "Ivy... Hunter... Sage. There's a theme here." She blushes and then whispers, "We should name our kids another shade of green."

I smirk, rolling on top of her in one swift move that makes her squeal in delight.

"How about Chartreuse?" I nuzzle the side of her neck, making her chuckle.

"What? No. That's awful," she replies.

"Then what about Lime?" I tease her ear with my teeth

and she shakes her head. "No? How about Mint? Pistachio? Oh, I know… Moss."

She laughs loudly, throwing her head back and giving me access to her throat. "Moss Sage? You're insane," she retorts, letting out a breathy moan as I nudge her entrance with my already steel-like cock.

She's most definitely sore, but I plan to take her slow and sweet, the thought of my child growing inside her belly making me want to make sweet love to her. "We already know that, lovely Ivy. I'm insane for you." I sink into her inch by inch, watching her face contort from ache to pleasure. "Seafoam?" I suggest playfully, and she shakes her head once more.

"I've got it," she murmurs, closing her eyes and taking me deep. "A few, actually."

"Tell me," I urge, circling my hips and making her whimper.

"Olive, Jade, or Emerald if we have a girl. And Forest, Viridian, or Hunter after you if it's a boy," she says, her legs locking around my hips.

"That's quite a few shades of green," I murmur against her neck as I thrust deep.

She giggles, making my cock jolt. "Fifty shades of green."

I shake my head, a smile covering my face as she opens her eyes to peek up at me. "A shade of green it is, lovely Ivy. Anything you want."

And as her eyes shimmer in complete happiness, we spend the night working on number one.

The End

AFTERWORD

Please take a moment to leave a short review. Every single one is greatly appreciated!

Join our reader groups on Facebook!

KD-Rob's Mob
https://www.facebook.com/groups/KDRobsMob/

CC Monroe's Yas Queens
https://www.facebook.com/groups/CCMonroesHoneys/

If you haven't read our first co-written book in our Dirty Doctors, make sure to check out Steal You, about a very naughty fertility doctor.

ALSO BY KD ROBICHAUX

THE BLOGGER DIARIES TRILOGY

Wished for You

Wish He Was You

Wish Come True

No Trespassing

CLUB ALIAS SERIES (STANDALONES)

Confession Duet (Before the Lie & Truth Revealed)

Seven

Mission: Accomplished

Knight

Scary Hot (Happily Ever Alpha World)

Doc (Coming Soon)

CO-WRITTEN WITH CC MONROE

Steal You

Number Neighbor

(More Dirty Doctors Coming Soon!)

All book links can be found on my website:
https://authorkdrobichaux.wixsite.com/authorkdrobichaux

Editing by Barb of Hot Tree Editing
www.hottreeediting.com

Cover Design by Cassy of Pink Ink Designs

www.pinkinkdesigns.com

ALSO BY CC MONROE

ALWAYS AND FOREVER SERIES
Always the One
Always Us
Forever the One
Forever Us

THE LOVING SERIES
Loving Ben Cooper
Loving Kate Beckett (Coming Soon)

CROSSOVER SERIES W/AURORA ROSE REYNOLDS
Until Kayla
Until Mercy

CO-WRITTEN WITH KD ROBICHAUX
Steal You
Number Neighbor
(More Dirty Doctors Coming Soon!)

Made in the USA
Monee, IL
01 January 2021